New Year's RESOLUTION

Babette Bailey

Mission: To Proclaim Transformation and Truth

Publisher: Transformed Publishing, Cocoa, FL

Website: www.transformedpublishing.com

Email: transformedpublishing@gmail.com

ISBN: 978-1-953241-55-9

DEDICATION

I would like to dedicate this book to all those who dare to dream; those who dare to believe in the good old fashioned "New Year's Resolution", and those ready for new beginnings.

We've heard many wonderful stories of how God can miraculously change lives; how love can come suddenly; and how God can turn our messes into messages. We've experienced those miracles, as well. Let's believe again.

If you are hopeful, if you are ready for a new beginning, if you are ready for inspiration, laughter, adventure, and even love, this book is dedicated to you. May you be filled with a newfound hope, passion, determination, inspiration, dedication, expectation, revelation, and more.

I'm asking one little thing if you don't mind. As you believe with me, pray with me for all who need a jump start to get their lives back on track, pep back in their step, and a new wind of inspiration to reach for their dreams. May they receive that and more.

ACKNOWLEDGEMENTS

I want to always acknowledge God for all the gifts, talents, provisions, opportunities, miracles, friendships, blessings and more, that He has given and continues to give us consistently. I want to acknowledge those who give and serve in Him through Him and for Him.

I want to acknowledge, once again, all who have supported me as I have strived to share my heart, my dreams, and the talents I feel God has given me to share with the world. Family, friends, associates, acquaintances, even those I have not had the pleasure of meeting - thank you.

I hope my striving and seeing my dreams fulfilled will encourage someone else to reach for their dreams. This may be a small seed, but who knows what it can produce when it is put into the right soil or the right hands. So, if anyone reading this book knows a producer or is a producer and can see this book turning into a movie that's my ultimate desire. Let's collaborate.

I also want to acknowledge my publisher who continues to go above and beyond to help me fulfill my dreams and to help keep the fire burning. To anyone who is thinking of writing and publishing your book, I highly recommend my publisher Mrs. Diana Robinson. She will make it happen once you get it into her hands.

TABLE OF CONTENTS

Introduction

Every year, we start thinking about what we want to do for the New Year; what things we want to leave in the old year, and what we want to see change in the New Year.

It is always exciting; we start the year off strong, on fire, focused, etc. Then, we either stay true to our goals and hit our targets, or we fall off due to distractions, discouragement, untimely goals, or maybe we just set the bar too high for our level of endurance.

No matter our past success or failure, this story is meant to reignite our passion to set those New Year's Resolutions again. It is meant to inspire us to believe we can reach our goals; provoke us to help and encourage one another; as well as touch our hearts with laughter, romance, and intrigue. I hope it will also impress within us a desire to invite God into our new goals and aspirations; believing that He is the difference maker in all our endeavors and desires.

Enjoy.

Babette Bailey

<u>*New Year's Resolution Tradition*</u>

Every year we're determined and revived in our minds

That some things are gonna have to change

There's something about the thought of a new year coming in

That helps us start working on those things

Whether it's just tradition, a ritual or a real thing

It has helped bring forth dreams long forgotten

It has sparked new hope and new inspiration

For people who had lost and misplaced their passions

So thank God for New Years and New Beginnings

And for New Year's Resolution traditions

I encourage everyone who has ever had a dream

That has slipped away, to get back to your mission

New books, new songs, new love, new moves

New strength, new determination, new whatever you want to do

New relationships with God, that's always a good place to start

A new determination to have a clean and pure heart

I hope just the thought of your new direction

Will give you the jump start you need

To get started moving again

And to never give up on your dreams

If you've made some mistakes that derailed you

Or you feel like it's just too late

I've heard testimonies of the things God has done

For those who dared to have faith

I'm daring you to believe you can; daring you to start anew

To strive for what you've always longed for

And always known you could do

I dare you to take the limits off of God

Totally believe there's nothing that He can't do

I dare you to start a New Year's Resolution tradition

Every year of being a better you

1

The Challenge

It was soon to be the first day of another year. All the guys were sitting around the crib, by the fire talking about their plans for the new year.

"Yo man, what are we gonna do different this year?" Bug asked. "I want to do something really challenging, different, fun, crazy, and wild too."

"Man, you do that every year. I think you should get ready to settle down and find you a wife to take care of your butt," K.T. told him.

"What? Like *that* one you almost married?" Serge joined in the teasing. "She was gonna take care of you alright. As long as you could afford to take care of her."

"I'm not trying to have any more expenses," Bug joked, laughing as K.T. popped him upside the head with a pillow.

"Man, every woman isn't like that. Maybe I'll get me one of them big women who can cook," K.T. said.

"Not during this time of year," Tipp added in. "You know every woman who's overweight is gonna be on a diet beginning on New Year's Day and at the gym every day after work instead of home cooking. You better wait a couple of months till they get passed that."

"That's what we need to do," said Serge. "Man, we haven't done anything since our football days."

"Okay, you jocks! I got just the thing for your New Year's Resolution," Coop finally added in after sitting back listening to everybody else. He sat up, getting everybody's attention. "It's challenging! Wild! Crazy! Fun! Like nothing we've ever done before." They all looked at Coop funny.

"No, Coop! These ideas you be having be too righteous for me," K.T. objected. "I mean I'm gonna go to church and all that, but you be talking about going to Egypt, and fasting for two and three months! I ain't with that!" They all laughed, even Coop.

"Ah man, you just don't know how to open your mind up to more than what your old rusty body is used to," Coop responded. "This idea I have is going to challenge you in every way - mentally, physically, socially, and yes, spiritually." Everybody sat up and leaned closer as Coop began to explain, "Check it out. First of all, we know there are going to be all kinds of women really desiring to lose weight. I say each of us pick one to help reach their goal." Intentionally looking at Serge, Coop continued, "Next, we're not allowed to have an affair with them or anyone while we're helping them."

"See! I knew he was gonna say something crazy!" K.T. interrupted. "No sex! For how long? And big women! And there's more!"

"Two months," Coop answered looking at K.T., as if the challenge was directed towards him, then turning to the others, "I got five hundred dollars that says you can't hang," Coop added.

"What? Deacon, you bettin'?" Serge asked Coop. "Something tells me this might be a real challenge! You think I can't control myself, don't you? That's what you're really trying to say! Man, I can't help it if the women be sweatin' me."

"So, what are you saying?" Coop asked Serge. "You saying you can?"

"I'm in," Serge confirmed, "and I'm gonna go to church every Sunday," he said calmly and confidently sitting back on the couch. "I'm ready for it. I might even get married this year."

"Yeah, right," Bug added. "But, okay. I'm in, too. It ain't no challenge if we ain't got to give up something. Plus, I like big women."

"But there's no liking going on. Not until after the two months is over," Coop reminded him, "Right?"

"I got it," Bug said. "Do you have the money?"

Coop didn't answer. He just looked at him and smiled.

"What about you, Tipp?" Bug asked. "You might have to get you a skinny lady and help her gain weight," he teased as they all laughed grabbing his big belly."

"Man, I can do this. We can get right together. Then we can understand what each other's going through." Tipp said.

"Man, that's deep," K.T. added digging for his wallet, "I'm in, too. But how big these women got to be?"

"At least two hundred pounds," Coop clarified, "and they've got to lose at least thirty pounds; fifteen for each month."

"Are you sure you can handle this, Serge? You know you're used to them California slims," Bug teased. "Well, what about you, Deacon?" Bug asked Coop, "You down too, right?"

"Sho', you right," Coop smirked, "only since I'm challenging you guys to remain sex free - you get to challenge me, for say, $200 apiece, your call."

"Okay!" Serge jumped in, "I say you have to pick the wildest woman we can find for those two months to help." They all laughed and sat back. "Man, I'm gonna find one of them pretty big ones, so when she loses that weight, she'll be *all that*," Serge said as if he could picture how fine she's gonna be.

"Well, let's do it," Coop agreed heading off to his room. "Oh, I almost forgot," Coop turned around to up the ante, "we've got to be in shape for the amateur tryouts by the end of February. We each have to make the first line picks at least. And the one who doesn't go all the way pays $100 to each of us."

"Yeah!" They all stood on their feet getting more excited.

The next morning, they all jumped into their cars and headed to the gym. As soon as they arrived, Serge and Bug both spotted an attractive lady with long pretty hair on the scale weighing herself. They looked at each other and rushed over to see what the scale showed.

203 pounds

Bug reached out and grabbed her hand, as she started to step off the scale, "Here, let me help you," he said kindly. "I'm June," he continued trying not to sound too goofy by saying 'Bug'. "What's your name?" he asked as he followed her over to the exercise bikes.

She smiled as she began to make conversation with him, "I'm Leah, but my friends call me Bunny." Bug smiled and winked his eye at Serge, as he continued his conversation from the bike beside her.

Serge went over to the treadmill and started walking. Just as he did, another young lady got on the one next to him. Still gazing at the lady with Bug, he hadn't noticed her, but K.T. did. As she turned to ask for help setting up the machine, Serge took notice. Abruptly, K.T. slipped right between them and offered *his* assistance. He began to make conversation with her and nonchalantly got on the treadmill on the other side of her.

"I'm K.T.," he said, "What's your name?"

"Thanks," she said, "I'm Gail."

Serge, starting to feel discouraged and defeated as he looked around at *who* was left, then slowed the treadmill down to scan the gym more carefully for a better opportunity. Another lady, coming from another station, walked up behind him. "Are you gonna use that thing or let somebody use it who needs it?" she questioned with a bold attitude, as if talking to everybody in the gym.

Serge automatically knew *this* was the one for Coop. He smiled as he stopped the machine and got off, "I'm done. Do you know how to use it, or do you need my friend here," motioning for Coop, "to help you?"

"What you think, I ain't never worked out before?" She responded with even more sass, "Don't worry I'm gonna lose this weight, Sugar. And don't you come trying to get with me when I do."

Serge laughed at Coop and backed away. Coop decided to back away for a few minutes to think things over.

Now with a game plan, Coop tried again to make a first impression, "My friend didn't mean to offend you, and, if he did, I apologize, for him." Coop said smoothly, "But he's right; if I can be of any assistance, please let me know. I'm Coop," he introduced himself in an attempt to win her acceptance.

As he turned to walk away, she called to him, "Excuse me, Coop, I'm Naomi. Thank you, and I'm gonna hold you to that now." Coop winked at her and headed for the bikes.

Tipp in the meantime, spotted a woman who caught his attention on the mats trying to do sit-ups. He kneeled down to hold her feet. "You wouldn't by any chance be looking for a workout partner, would you?" Tipp inquired.

She sat up for a moment, "Are you serious?" she asked almost laughing, "Sure! Especially if you can help keep me motivated. I'm Elaine."

"I'm Tipp," he responded politely.

"So, when do we start?"

"How about today?" Tipp proposed.

"Perfect," Elaine agreed and continued her sit-ups.

"I'll talk while you concentrate - tell you a little about me; then I want to hear about you," Tipp suggested, and the conversation began.

Meanwhile, Serge moved over to the weights area. His eyes were immediately drawn to a nice, *very* nice, looking lady lifting weights across from him. But she didn't look overweight, so he tried not to look. Nevertheless, she was too beautiful to ignore. She paid him no attention and continued her workout. She stood up to move to the next station and Serge couldn't help but notice her hips. They were huge considering her small upper frame which was all he could see at first. He tried not to stare, as he purposely maneuvered toward her to make conversation, "You come here often?" was Serge's opening line.

She didn't respond. Obviously, she wasn't buying his lame attempt to spark her interest.

"You come here often?" he repeated.

"No!" she responded short and to the point.

"Just started?" he asked trying to be persistent.

"Yes," she snapped, again short and to the point.

"Dog, why so cold, Baby? Is it me or are you just angry with the world?" he asked her both jokingly and genuinely awaiting her response.

"I guess I'm just *not* about the game right now. I'm trying to focus on getting this new year started off right," she explained, ready to shut down the dialogue, "and men aren't on the list! I don't feel like dealing with any! Not even you!" She abruptly walked away, leaving behind her towel.

"So, is that forever or just for a little while?" he pestered, as he picked up her towel and trailed behind her.

"I don't know," she blurted out, not feeling as if she owed him any type of explanation.

"Well, would you consider me if you change your mind? I'll be here every day about this time," he asked as he attempted to keep the conversation going and playfully returned her towel into her hand. He smiled, hoping to get one in return, and introduced himself, "I'm Serge."

"Thank you," she replied as she grabbed her towel back, without returning the smile.

2

The New Begins

Soon they all returned to the crib with names of their new friends and hopes of meeting their challenges. Well, everyone except Serge but he was determined to win over his prospect. The truth is that's not really what bothered him the most. His ego was crushed. He wasn't used to being rejected. They all took showers and headed off to work.

That evening, they sat around for a few minutes joking with each other. Serge was sitting at the table picking over his dinner when his phone rang. It was one of his old female friends calling to see if he wanted to hang out for the evening. As much as that would have helped him right then, he turned her down.

"I'm sorry, Baby. I'm not gonna be going out for a while. I got something going on," Serge told her, "but thanks for calling."

"Okay," she responded, and they hung up.

Serge cleared his plate and headed for bed. The other guys just looked at each other with eyebrows raised. Tired too, they all decided to call it a night.

The next day Serge woke up with renewed spirits. He woke everybody up in the house playing his music loudly and singing.

Bug got up firing off the questions to Serge, "What did you do, man? Slip out of the house last night and go on that date after all?"

"No, I just feel really lucky today."

"How lucky can you get?" Bug asked him, looking a bit depressed.

"Five hundred dollars' worth," Serge assured. "I'm gonna do this," he said energetically. "I'm not gonna focus on sex or failure or nothing that could defeat me. I'm not even gonna concentrate on the money. I'm gonna do it because I can." He brushed the waves in his hair and handed the brush to Bug, giving him the bathroom, then went back to his room, and turned the music up until everyone in the house was awake singing.

They were all dressed and ready to head out for work when Tipp came through the front door.

"Man, where you been, Tipp?" K.T. asked.

"Working out with Elaine," he hollered as he rushed upstairs to get ready for work.

They looked at each other and continued on.

After work they all felt their muscles ache as they changed their clothes and headed to the gym.

"Man, what are we supposed to be gaining from all this anyway?" Bug complained, "Besides about seven hundred dollars? Are we gonna end up hurting these women in the end? I think we should have thought about this thing a little more. Cause I'm not trying to have no fatal repercussions. You know what I'm saying?"

"Just be honest," Coop told him. "If you're not taking advantage of her and not leading her to think it's more than it is you shouldn't have to worry about that, right?"

"Man, you know how these women are. Even when you tell them straight up, they still fall in love with you. I don't know about this thing man," Bug continued.

"Let's go. Bring your scary butt on," K.T. urged teasing and grabbing Bug by the head, "you old, mama's boy!"

"Wait," Bug said, as he grabbed the guys by the hand, "let's have a word of prayer before we go. Come on Coop, pray for us man!"

Coop agreed. He said a prayer for all of them; then prayed especially for Bug, and they headed out the door.

When they arrived at the gym, the women were already there, at different stations. Serge went right to work trying to win over his new *friend*. He had a plan. He found out her name from the guy who worked at the check-in desk and slipped into action.

"So, what's up Ms. Adderly?" he asked. "How are you doing, this beautiful day?"

She proudly ignored him.

Serge wasn't deterred and continued, "Man, you ain't no better than yesterday. Well, that's alright. I got a plan. I figure we can both reach our goals in two months or less if you're up for fighting to reach your goal as hard as you're fighting me. Now, my goal is to be in *that* football shape I used to be in back in the day. I am even trying out for the amateur league once I am ready. What's your goal?"

She finally stopped long enough to acknowledge him, "Look Mr. Whoever you are, all I want to do is chill for a while. I don't want no help, no man, no plan, nothing you got to give. Why can't you see I just want to be left alone?"

He looked at her for a moment, questioning his own sanity. For a moment, he was really afraid and thought he better leave her alone. But he couldn't give up, "Nope, for whatever reason, we were meant to meet, and I intend on finding out what that reason is. Just workout with me. Let's strive for our goals and help each other. I promise not to hit on you – *try* not to hit on you, I mean. Well, until we've reached our goal that is. Deal?"

"You promise?" she finally said, then added, "No, you've got to put more than that on the line."

"Okay!" Serge smiled, glad to hear his negotiations were getting him somewhere, "Whatever you say."

"Okay!" she agreed, "Is that your fine sports car parked outside? The black one with the playboy on the front?"

"Yeah," he said looking at her as if she had lost her mind.

"Well, here is my stipulation. If you hit on me any time during these two months, I keep your precious sports car for a weekend, okay?"

"Oh," he said relaxing, "I thought you were going to say *have*. But yeah, okay, we can do that. But what about if I don't hit on you? I got to get something for being so good, don't I?"

"Name it," she said confidently.

That scared him. He didn't know what to say. She threw his whole game plan off by saying that. "What are you trying to say?" he asked to clarify, "I can have whatever I name?"

"Anything," she assured.

He thought for a minute, and asked, "Can I name it when the time is up?"

"Okay," she agreed, "if you make it."

"I can deal with that," Serge confirmed.

"So, let's hear this plan," she said as she leaned forward finally smiling.

"Hey! You can't be teasing a brother and all that now, wearing all kinds of tight clothes and all that other stuff either, or smiling and getting all close," he went on, as he unfolded a piece of paper from his pocket. He already had a written plan and began to explain it to his new workout partner.

* * *

Meanwhile, Coop was doing his thing and talking to Naomi, "I believe most of our success begins in our heart and mind. If we can change the way we think and feel, we can change the way we act, and the things we do. Are you up for that kind of challenge?"

"You must be planning on being around for a while? Those kinds of changes take some time," Naomi added.

Coop worked to secure her commitment, "They're challenging, too. So, I guess it depends on whether you're up for the challenge."

As quietly as she'd probably ever spoken in her life, Naomi uttered, "I think so."

"Okay! What do you say we talk over a nice, healthy smoothie?"

"Let's go!" Naomi affirmed. They grabbed their gear and headed out.

* * *

Bug was busy working out with Bunny.

"What's up?" Bunny asked, "You seem distracted today.

"I'm okay."

"If you don't feel like working out. . ." Bunny started to say.

But Bug interrupted her, "Look Bunny, I got to be honest with you, okay? I don't know where this is leading. I'd like to work out with you and get to know you, but I guess I feel like I'm kinda leading you on or something. I don't want there to be any misleading, anybody hurt, just a good friendship to come about, while we both reach our goals, and I figure we can both really help each other."

"I can deal with that," she assured, smiling, "I appreciate your honesty. Now, will you please relax? You're starting to make me tense."

He laughed, "Okay. Put that thing on fifteen minutes and let's get busy." As he moved, he grunted, "Oh! It hurts so good," feeling the soreness from the day before.

* * *

K.T. and Gail seemed to be hitting it off really well. They both enjoyed walking so they headed for the treadmills. Fifteen minutes into their hike to nowhere, K.T.

asked, "What do you say, let's take this thing outside, add some scenery? If you really enjoy walking, maybe even go to the beach. You can wear your 'kini," he teased.

"I will wear one, if you will," she teased him back. "But, besides the 'kini, that's an excellent idea. Let's go!"

They agreed to leave their stuff in their cars and headed down the street.

"So, what's your goal?" K.T. asked.

"You know," Gail answered, "the old New Year's Resolution tradition. Don't really have a plan; just want to start working out and eating good, trying to get that old high school figure back."

"I hear you. My homies and I are planning to get in shape for the amateur tryouts at the end of February. So, I'm really going to have to run, lift weights, sit-ups, push-ups, all that. You down for a workout, that tough?"

"Am I!" Gail affirmed, "You must be the help I've been praying for. I'm all for strict discipline and working out."

"There's one thing though," K.T. explained, "nothing personal, but while I'm in training I can't be distracted or going through any mental challenges, so don't be trying to seduce me or nothing."

They both laughed.

"I'm gonna be as straight as you," she told him.

"And you have to promise not to be offended if I get too hard on you." K.T. cautioned.

"Oh, I'm going to be the one who's gonna have the whistle," she told him. "You're the one who's gonna have to run; for time, up-hill and all that. Yeah, the beach will be good for you. What do you say we hit the beach about 5:30 every morning, run a couple miles, and do weights in the evening after work?"

"Girl, you must be the help I've been praying for, too!"

"Oh, you haven't heard the way you gotta run yet," she said laughing.

"What? I'm in there. Whatever it is I'm sure I can handle it." K.T. responded confidently.

The next morning, K.T. and Gail were true to their word and made it to the beach for an early run. First, she challenged him to run backwards.

"What, run backwards?" he mocked as he started jogging backwards. "Come on, let's see what you got."

Now, jogging face to face, they continued their playful dialogue, "Oh, don't let this big butt fool you now. I used to run track in school. I still got a little bit. And I'm gonna get better and faster. I might have you run sprints with me on your back, just to get your speed up," she told him, and he started blushing.

They ran for a little while longer, then they started to head back. "So, what position do you play anyway?" she asked.

That conversation led back to their high school days and before they knew it, they were back to their vehicles. He walked her to her car, and they agreed on the time they would meet for their evening workout.

* * *

Tipp and Elaine met for their weight workout in the evenings also. They both were sore from working out the day before but determined to stick to their commitment. Elaine massaged Tipp's muscles a little as they loosened up on the mats and he massaged hers. Next, they did their sit-ups and stretches, push-ups and bends. Then they worked out with the weights. After their workout, Tipp drove her home. They hung outside and talked for about an hour, about any and everything. They both hadn't gotten used to working out yet, so they were equally tired, and decided to call it an evening.

3

Staying Focused

Elaine had already begun to have feelings for Tipp. She went inside, took a shower, and fixed herself up really nice in preparation for the glorious day when he would ask her out. She danced around in the mirror and sang for a little while then one of her friends called. Elaine was reluctant to tell her about Tipp since nothing had officially developed *yet*, but she couldn't resist. Elaine was excited she had someone in her life like Tipp. She told her friend all she knew and thought she knew. Her friend said she was happy for her but something in her voice didn't sound right. Elaine asked, "What's wrong, Teesie? You don't sound happy at all for me."

"I am Elaine, but please make sure he's serious before you fall in love. I know it's exciting and you're happy and I'm so glad things look so good, but I don't want to see you hurt again."

"You're right," Elaine agreed, calming down. "I'm gonna just try to enjoy the friendship and not get caught up. Thanks, girl. So, what's up with you and Benny?"

"I gave up," Teesie admitted, "I'm tired, girl! I can't *see* it anymore. I love him, but either he doesn't know what love is, or he just doesn't love me; still playing them same old games. And he was all for us parting ways, so I knew it was time. I haven't seen him in about four weeks."

"Do you miss him?" Elaine asked.

"Sometimes. But I was unhappy with him, and I don't miss him enough to go back to *that*. Maybe I'll go to your gym and find me a good-looking workout partner," Teesie pondered, now laughing.

"Just don't be looking at Tipp," Elaine declared.

"Ah girl, you know I'm not down with that game. I love you too much."

"I know," Elaine agreed, "I love you, too. But right now, I gotsta go get my beauty sleep."

They laughed and exchanged good-byes.

★ ★ ★

The next morning, all the guys were up at 5 am. Everyone had started working out in the mornings, as well as the afternoons.

Coop and Naomi had agreed to a morning devotional and prayer together over the phone Coop called, as scheduled, and Naomi was ready with her Bible in hand. They read a few verses Coop had picked out and discussed them. Coop prayed for them both and they were done.

"That was very different than anything I'm used to doing," Naomi told Coop, "I mean, I believe in God of course, but I guess I've never really been a religious person. It kind of makes me feel different, but in a good way. 'We can do all things through Christ who strengthens us'," she quoted from memory, "I guess I better start reading a little bit more. I need all this positive stuff."

"Well, Naomi, that's what I'm about, so if you need any help, call me. Think about coming to our Bible study too, every Friday night," Coop offered.

"Now, that would be a change. Going to church instead of going to the club. I think the Lord sent you in my direction for more than one reason. I have actually been thinking a lot about going to church and really changing the way I live. Friday night, you say?" she confirmed.

"Yeah."

"At what time?" she asked.

"Seven o'clock."

"Okay, and thanks Coop, I really appreciate all your help and I'll see you this evening, right?"

"Five o'clock," he replied then they exchanged good-byes.

* * *

Tipp rushed over to pick up Elaine and she was still in bed. He banged on the door until she woke up. Realizing she had overslept; she threw on her robe and let him in. In a hurry, she rushed back to her room apologizing and put on her warm-ups. She didn't bother putting on her shoes. She just grabbed them and told him she'd put them on in the car.

He grabbed her by the arm as she rushed for the door, "Hey, it's okay. Elaine, slow down. Wait for me before you start the workout," he told her, jokingly, "Go ahead and put your shoes on. That ground is cold."

Finally, Elaine took a deep breath, sat down, and started putting her shoes on. "I look kind of crazy, just waking up, huh?" she asked him.

"You look beautiful," he expressed, "Your hair is sticking up a little bit, but it's cute."

"You're teasing me?" she questioned.

"You're beautiful," he told her again.

She couldn't help blushing as they headed out the door. Even after they got into the car she was still blushing, "See, why did you have to go and embarrass me? Now, I'm gonna be acting goofy," she honestly expressed.

"Good, now we're even," he said, "because I feel kind of goofy myself."

"Why do you feel goofy?" Elaine asked the man who appeared to have no imperfections.

"I guess I just feel funny trying to work out and run being as heavy as I am. You know what I mean?" he asked her.

"I know exactly what you mean," she related. "But weight on men is attractive, I think."

"Yeah?" he asked smiling, "So, I'm kind of alright?" he added laughing even more.

"From what I see and have seen in you, Tipp, you're a beautiful man."

"Hey! Watch out now," he playfully scolded, "just say I'm all that or something. Don't be calling me beautiful."

"Well," she looked deeper into him, "I think you're all that."

They both got really quiet for a moment as if they were thinking a little more seriously.

"Thank you," he said, "I needed to hear that."

"Me, too."

They arrived at the park, got out, did their stretches, and were on their way. They alternated between running and walking, and made it through the two-mile course, then headed back. The sun was just coming up as they returned to Elaine's house.

"Man, I wish we could just hang out and enjoy this sunrise," she whispered, before she realized what she was saying. She squinted her eyes shut feeling like she was obviously moving too fast.

"How about Saturday morning?" he asked her. "We can bring a blanket out to the park and after we work out just chill for a bit."

"Sounds beautiful," she looked at him as if she wanted to give him a kiss. Then Elaine thought about what Teesie had said, so she smiled and said good-bye.

His thoughts were along the same lines, so he returned the smile and the good-bye. As he drove off, he had to slap himself for the thoughts he was having. He wasn't even through the first week and he was having thoughts of being intimate. She was a little heavy, but she was beautiful.

* * *

When Tipp got back to the house, Coop was sitting at the table. Tipp sat down with him, not saying a word. Coop could feel the tension coming from Tipp and just began to laugh.

"What are you laughing at?" Tipp asked him.

"Man, I can't believe you're breaking already. You know what you'll have to do, don't you?" Coop asked him.

Tipp didn't say anything; just looked at him.

Coop went on, "You'll have to make sure someone is always around you when you see her. Otherwise, the temptation is going to get greater each time you're alone. So, you're really feeling this chick, huh?"

"I'm enjoying this whole adventure," Tipp admitted. "Working out, helping someone else, making a good friend, and looking forward to different things. I do feel like I'm developing feelings already, especially when she looks at me the way she does – sometimes, like she could rock my world," he added laughing.

"Listen, Tipp, slow down man," Coop reminded, "You haven't known this chick enough time. Sex often draws a man into a commitment or a relationship that he doesn't want to be in after he's in it. If it's more than that, then go for it, but don't let lust commit you. Find out if your goals are the same, your interests, your views on life, raising kids, and if you two are even compatible. Then go from there. Man, sex is a commitment. Once you do it, you're gonna be expected to do a lot more than work out. Just make sure, that's all I'm saying," Coop paused.

Tipp did not respond, but it was apparent he was listening, so Coop continued, "If you are not ready to put *the* ring on her finger, don't go all the way. Somebody may end up getting hurt. The Word of God tells us to abstain anyway till marriage, and we can see there are good reasons behind that. I'm not gonna act like I haven't been tempted. I have," Coop admitted, "So, I know how you feel, but I know in my heart He will bless me because I'm being obedient. And if I feel like I can't wait any more, then I'll prepare to marry. The Word of God also tells us it's better to marry than to burn."

Tipp interrupted him, "You're right man. I'm sure it's just the lust thing at this point." He slapped Coop some dap and headed for the shower.

* * *

K.T. had been thinking about what kind of workout Gail had in store for him. Whatever it was, he was confidently up for the challenge. He picked her up on schedule and didn't even have to park the car. She ran outside as soon as he pulled up, and they headed for the beach. She had a big tote bag with her and of course he asked what it was for. She pulled out a pair of leg weights, "Just consider me your personal trainer," she said. "First we're gonna have you jog a little while with these on to build up your legs for speed, plus I will be able to keep up with you. Then," she continued reaching in the bag again, pulling out a football, "we're gonna see what you got. And don't worry about seeing good, I got some glow in the dark tape, too," she assured and started taping the football up.

"You got your little stuff together, huh?" he smiled and looked impressed. "I like that. If I didn't know any better, I'd think you knew a little bit about the game."

"I do," she told him, "and I can play."

"Play what?" he teased.

"I was talking about football. I can catch, I can throw, and I know how to play the game," she informed him full of laugher.

"Talk is cheap! You're gonna have to show me," K.T. insisted.

They enjoyed the drive and arrived at the beach. He exited the car, walked to the passenger door, and opened it. Instead of a 'thank you', Gail abruptly handed him the weights, "Here you go!"

They stretched a little bit, then they were off.

"Okay," she said to him, as they were running, "every time I blow my whistle, you've got to sprint ahead, then back when I blow it again. Ready?" she shouted and blew the whistle before he had a chance to speak.

"No, I'm not ready," he delayed. "You're trying to kill me!"

"Come on now," she jested. "You know them coaches used to put it on you guys when you were in high school. Don't wimp out on me now. Go!" she demanded, blowing the whistle again.

He sprinted forward, until Gail blew the whistle again for him to come back. They jogged a little bit further as she explained the next drill, "This time, when I blow, I want you to run with high knees until I blow it again."

Immediately, Gail blew the whistle. K.T. tried to speak, but she started yelling, "Get 'em up! Let's go!"

He obeyed, yet she yelled louder, "Higher!"

When she was satisfied, she blew the whistle again for him to return to his normal jog.

"I believe you could be a coach for real," he told her.

"Are you alright?" she asked him.

"Yeah," he assured her.

"I'm not gonna kill you, but this time, I want you to jog backwards. Then we're gonna come back doing the same thing, okay?" she asked him.

This time she awaited his response. "Okay," K.T. agreed.

Gail blew the whistle. He turned and started jogging backwards. It seemed to K.T. like she would never blow the whistle again. "Hey! What's up with the whistle?" he cried out. "That thing stopped working," he complained.

Finally, she blew it again and he turned around.

"If you stopped using so much energy whining, you'd be alright. What's up? Are you up for this or are you one of those guys who's always whining to the referee on the field? Come on, tough guy! Go!" she hollered again as she blew the whistle.

He jogged backwards for the duration of time in between the two whistles, without saying a word.

"Alright!" Gail energetically encouraged K.T., "That's what I'm talking about. You're in better shape than I thought."

"You, too. I'm impressed. I can't wait to see that arm."

Without allowing much rest, Gail blew the whistle again, "Back to high knees! High knees, get 'em up!"

"That's as high as . . .," he started to say before he caught himself whining again.

Soon, she blew the whistle again and shouted, "No break! Change directions. Backwards!"

He had his eyes closed, as the workout was getting tougher and tougher. He didn't realize she had stopped jogging until he heard the whistle blow again. K.T. opened his eyes and the football was coming straight for his face. Instinctively, he caught it and looked to see where Gail was.

"Good throw!" he hollered as he looked to make sure it wasn't someone else who threw the ball.

Without warning, he shot it right back at her. She caught it hard in the chest, "Ouch," she screamed bending to the ground.

He ran over to see if she was alright.

"I'm alright," Gail assured, trying to stay pumped, "You just drop those weights, let's see what you got."

He took the weights off and it was on.

"Go left about four feet, cut right, then stop, got it?" she directed.

K.T. nodded.

"Down, set, hike."

On command, K.T. took off to run the play. When he stopped and turned around, she put it right in his chest, "Good gracious!" he shouted.

"Alright, your turn," K.T. gestured to Gail as he explained, "We're going for the bomb. Go long, and on the count of five, counting slow, look for the ball."

She ran counting slowly to herself, *1, 2, 3, 4, 5.* Then she looked up. The ball was right above her, on schedule. She caught it. "Good arm!" she complimented, "I'm totally impressed. How'd you know I was at *five?*"

K.T. shrugged his shoulders and smirked, "What can I say?"

She looked at her watch and realized the time had slipped away from them. "We better go," she said trying to keep the disappointment out of her voice.

They ran back to the car. The workout ended, but the conversation continued as they drove away.

"That was excellent," K.T. emphasized. "Beat running on that treadmill, didn't it?"

"Indeed!"

"But what are we going to do about our evenings?" he inquired.

"I know you're not hitting on me," she teased.

"No! Don't even try it," he contested. "I'm just thinking we need to work out in the evenings, too."

"What do you say we hit the weights or go for a swim, sometimes?" Gail suggested.

"I think that's perfect," K.T. confirmed. "So, what time should I pick you up?"

"How about six o'clock?" she suggested.

"Six, it is then."

He dropped her off and drove away, keeping his eyes aimed at the rearview mirror until Gail was no longer in sight.

⋆ ⋆ ⋆

Tipp and Bug were coming in about the same time.

"What happened to you?" Bug asked K.T. "Is that girl working you or you working her?"

"Man, *that* girl had me aired out. It's all good though. I got to get it right. I'm gonna make that team," K.T. said confidently.

"Yeah." Bug challenged, "What do you say we see what you got next weekend - Saturday morning? Let's all get together."

"I don't know man," K.T. teased, "I've got to check with my trainer."

"Why don't you bring her along?" Bug suggested.

Overhearing their conversation, Tipp added, "We can invite all the ladies. Let them cheer for us."

K.T. laughed, "They might be doing more than cheering."

They all rushed to get ready for work and headed out the door.

4

Emotional Shifts

Saturday morning came for Tipp and Elaine to enjoy their sunrise. After their morning beach workout, Elaine routinely followed Tipp back to the car.

"What are we doing?" Elaine asked, "I thought we were going to hang out this morning."

"Ah man!" Tipp explained, "I completely forgot. I didn't even bring a blanket."

"That's okay," she said trying to *not* sound disappointed.

"We can share my jacket, though" he said pulling it out from the back seat, "if you don't mind."

She started to feel funny, "You don't really want to hang out anymore, do you?" she asked him directly.

"Yes, I still want to," he said. "Come on!"

They found a nice spot, spread Tipp's jacket out, laid down, and looked into the sky. It had already begun to turn all sorts of beautiful colors. They both laid still for a few minutes, not saying anything.

"Do you believe in God?" Tipp asked unexpectedly.

"Of course!" Elaine answered. "Don't you?"

"Yes. Unfortunately, I haven't been going to church and everything like I should," Tipp confided, "but I'd like to go tomorrow. Would you come with me?"

"Sure! How about I cook us a nice dinner afterwards," Elaine offered.

"You're not supposed to cook on Sunday," he told her.

"You're not supposed to work on Sunday!" Elaine corrected. "And that's not work. I love to cook."

"Yeah!" Tipp agreed giving Elaine a big smile. "That's great, but you got to prepare something low-cal. I want to stay on my diet."

"Me too," she told him. "You're a hard person to read, you know that?"

Tipp pondered Elaine's observation for a moment and asked, "Why do you say that?"

She turned to face him, "You keep me so off balance. One minute I think you might like me. The next, I don't know what to think."

Tipp paused to process his thoughts before looking over at her. He tried to speak, but the words wouldn't come. He dropped his head on her shoulder and was quiet. Elaine didn't know what to think, so she matched Tipp's silence.

Finally, Tipp expressed himself, "I'm happy. Happier than I've been in a long time. I enjoy your company very much; *too much, sometimes.* It's kind of scary. I like you, my friend. I like you a whole lot! I guess, I just want to be sure it's *you* I like, and that I know you well enough to be able to say so without a doubt. I don't want to be in lust which fades. I don't want to get in deeper than I should have because I moved too fast." He reached over and stroked her arm, "I like you, Elaine."

"I like you, too, Tipp. And I get scared, too," she leaned her head into his and he held her in his arms for a while.

The sun continued to fluctuate through a spectrum of colors. Everything was beautiful. They laid there peacefully, without saying anything, just enjoying each other's company, and the rising of the sun.

"Man, I could stay here all day, but I guess we better go take showers and get changed if we're going out for breakfast," Tipp said looking to Elaine for a response.

"Sounds good to me," she said.

They finalized the plan, then went to their individual homes to shower and get ready for the next part of their day.

* * *

Meanwhile, Bug woke K.T. up to see if he and Gail were still going to the park with him and Bunny.

"Ah man! I didn't even mention it to her," K.T. regretted. "Maybe we'll meet you guys out there later. I'll give her a call and see what she's doing."

That wasn't going to stop Bug. He finished getting dressed. With his fresh haircut, new short set, and good smelling cologne, he was ready to go, but he felt like he was going on a date. He didn't know whether to dress down and wash off the cologne or what. Looking in the mirror, Bug asked himself, "Why you trippin'? You have always dressed nice and kept yourself looking good!" Finally, he convinced himself to go as he was and headed for the door.

"Who are you going out with?" Serge asked Bug.

"I'm not going out with anybody," Bug responded, as if he was upset Serge even asked.

"What's up with you, Bug? I'm just implying you're looking kind of good to be hanging around the house or with the fellas."

"Man, this girl makes me nervous! I don't know what to wear, where to go, how to act. I've never been like this before! And I don't understand it. Maybe I'll just go ahead and give up the five hundred dollars and be done with this. I should call her and cancel today," Bug bounced from thought to thought.

"Dog, man!" Serge asserted, "What's up with you? Is it the girl, not being able to handle the challenge of not dating, all the exercise, or what?"

Bug sat down for a minute and leaned back, taking a deep breath, "I'm tripping, huh?"

"You know you're trippin'," Serge affirmed. "The question is *why?*"

"I don't know," Bug admitted, "I guess I kind of feel like I'm committed somewhat."

"You are, but you're not married," Serge told him. "It's not the same kind of commitment. You're committed to the challenge we've all taken on. And I admit, this is probably the toughest one we've faced; besides the time we went camping for two weeks," he said with added humor.

They both laughed. "Yeah man, that was a trip, wasn't it?" Bug reminisced.

"Bug, don't let yourself go off the deep end behind this," Serge told him. "I don't care if you fail with the girl, but you better be on that football field."

"Yeah!" Bug responded and his excitement returned.

He rushed out the door, looked at his watch, and realized he was already thirty minutes late to pick up Bunny. Anticipating he would make it to her house soon, he didn't call to say he was running late.

By the time he got there, Bunny had changed her mind about going. She *thought* she sensed something by the way he had been acting, but today topped it off, "Listen Bug, if I remember correctly, you approached me. I didn't approach you. But this *friendship* thing doesn't seem to be working out. You seem to think I want something from you. To tell you the truth, it's starting to make me a little uneasy."

Bug leaned against the side of her door as they stood on the porch, "I'm sorry, Bunny. I don't know what's been going on with me. But it's not you, okay?"

"Okay, I'll talk to you later then," she concluded as she reached to close the door.

"Bunny, can I come in for a minute at least?"

"Let's just call it all off," she suggested. "I'm fine with it."

"Bunny, I don't want to call it off," Bug expressed with endearment in his voice.

"I do!" she insisted, "It's not working out for me."

"Will you at least think about reconsidering, Bunny?"

"Sure, but I need *my* time," she replied.

"Can I call you later?" Bug asked, not wanting to leave with things stagnant.

"Sure," she muttered and closed the door.

Now, he really felt bad. He leaned against the door for a minute as her words played through his mind. Not wanting to leave full of misunderstanding and uncertainty, Bug knocked on the door again.

He anticipated Bunny opening the door and waited a few minutes. Knowing she was there, but choosing not to respond, ignited Bug's regret.

Eventually, accepting the fact that Bunny wasn't going to answer, Bug got into his car and drove away.

He ended up at the gym where he used to box. He worked out on all the bags and the jump rope. He festered up a good sweat but was still upset with himself. His intentions were not to hurt anyone. But he felt as if he had.

* * *

Bunny went on an eating binge. She felt bad about herself. Rejection was her trigger. Even though Bug told her it wasn't her, she felt that it was. She sat down with a box of cereal and milk and wrapped herself in her blanket. After she had eaten the entire box, she cried. She cried until she fell asleep.

A few hours later the phone woke her up, but she didn't answer it. Realizing it was Bug, she checked her voicemail. She intensely listened to his voice, "Bunny, please call me," he pleaded, "please!" he said again before hanging up.

Overwhelmed, Bunny laid back on her pillow and battled her own thoughts:

Why does he keep messing with me? Maybe I'll just put on another two hundred pounds, then I never have to even worry about men.

Now, snuggled up close to her pillow, Bunny sought comfort she couldn't find. The phone rang again. This time there was no message, just a dial tone. She got up and headed for the kitchen, again. Fortunately, she didn't have much food. She knew if she had it, she would be tempted to eat it. Up to his point, Bunny was very committed to embracing a healthier lifestyle.

Emotional turmoil, set ablaze by discouragement, rejection, disappointment, and other torturous thoughts, manipulated Bunny to go out for ice cream. She didn't bother to do anything to fix herself up. Bunny grabbed her purse and keys and was off.

Just as she got to the door, Bug pulled up. He could see she was still upset so he ran to the car before she had a chance to get in, leaving his car in the road, "Baby, please! Can I talk to you?"

She couldn't help breaking down. She leaned her head against the car and started to cry. He wrapped his arms around her, held her, and kissed her on her head. He couldn't apologize enough. Finally, he took her back inside the house, then quickly ran back outside to park his car, and returned to comfort Bunny.

"Look, you don't owe me anything," she told him.

"Baby, I know. But for whatever reason, it hurts me to think I've hurt you. I care about you, Bunny. I guess I could feel more growing than was supposed to be there. Maybe that's why I've been so messed up lately; trying to keep myself under control," Bug confided.

"I don't need this. I don't know how I got in this predicament. My New Year's Resolution was to get myself where I want to be mentally, physically, socially, and spiritually, *not* get into a relationship," Bunny contested.

"Sometimes it's when you're not planning it that *it* happens," Bug assured.

He sat back down beside her and pulled her into his arms. "Please!" she said, "Don't make things any worse."

"I'm not," Bug responded, kissing her now on her face. "Can I be totally honest with you?"

"Please, do."

Bug cleared his throat and began, "Every year, me and the guys I live with find something to challenge us for our New Year's Resolution. This year, our challenge was like 3-in-1. We planned to find women wanting to get in shape, motivate them, and help them, meanwhile we were also training ourselves to make the amateur football team." He paused for a minute, then continued, "The third part," he said with a big sigh, "was that we couldn't get *involved* while we were helping these women out. I think the challenge may have been a little more than I can handle. I guess that's part of the reason I've been acting strange. The other part is, I'm just down-right scared. The truth is, I really like you. I like the person inside and that overrides whatever little flaws you may have on the outside. You're a little heavy, especially according to what I have been accustomed to, but you're beautiful. You have beautiful skin," he complimented rubbing her arms, "beautiful hair," he added, moving his hands to her hair, "a beautiful heart," he said with a kiss, "and a beautiful smile. I've had so much fun since we've been hanging out. I'm not used to that. So, I guess I was feeling too much, especially so soon. Will you please forgive me? Will you go on a date with me?"

"What about your challenge?"

"I don't care. I couldn't enjoy it if I did win. Besides, I'm not totally giving up; just the date part. I still plan on making the amateur football team, and helping the girl I chose reach her goal. That is, *if* she'll forgive me," Bug reiterated, looking into her face for a smile.

"She might, *if* you take her to the new movie she's been wanting to see," Bunny countered.

"How soon do you think *she* can be ready?" Bug teased.

"Ten minutes."

"I'll wait right here," he replied, leaning back down on the couch.

While he waited, Bug noticed the pictures that were placed around the house. Then he found a photo album, picked it up, and began looking through it. He smiled and laughed to himself as he saw pictures from when Bunny was a toddler up through high school. Soon she was ready.

Bunny was dressed up, looking more beautiful than he had realized she really was.

"I hope you don't mind if I run by the house and freshen up, too? You look too good for me to be going like this. As a matter of fact, you look too good to be going to *just* a movie. What do you say we grab a little dinner first?"

"Thanks, but no thanks. If you knew what I've eaten, you wouldn't be too pleased with me," Bunny replied.

Bug assured her, "I wouldn't be upset either. Especially, since I know it was my fault. Why do women go on them eating binges anyway when they get upset?" he asked.

"The same reason guys run away from their feelings," she told him, sarcastically.

"Okay, I'll buy that," he agreed, leaving the issue alone.

When they got to his house, no one was there. He brought her in, and she waited what seemed like only five minutes for him to shower and get dressed.

"Man! If I ever get showered and dressed that fast, I would be scared of myself. And you look great, Bug! I've been trying not to say anything too flattering since we were on restriction, but now that we're off, you are one good-looking man!" Bunny declared. "No wonder you're not married. Just kind of had your pick, huh?" she nudged.

"It wasn't like that," he said, going from being embarrassed, to serious.

"Please, that's what all of you guys say."

"Okay, I admit I was a little wild, but I've settled down," Bug shared as he opened the door for her, and they headed for the car.

He was a perfect gentleman the whole night; he opened doors, was careful to walk beside her and not in front of her, and offered to buy her little things along the way.

After their dinner and movie, they went for a walk on the beach. They stood on the pier for a while, and as it started getting colder, they found the excuse they wanted to hold each other. Even embraced in one another's arms, they couldn't take it anymore, it had gotten too cold, so they left.

As Bug drove Bunny back to her place, she tried to find the courage to ask him to stay for a while. Finally, just before she got out of the car, she turned and asked him if he wanted to call it a night or stay up and watch a movie.

"I'd really like to just cuddle a little while," he admitted, "whether we watch a movie or talk."

"Me too," she said smiling.

They ended up finding a good movie to watch. He told her about his friend Coop and how Coop talked to him about respecting women's bodies and not becoming involved in sexual relations until marriage, "As much as I want to do more than just hold you, I can't. Coop's words have stayed in my head," he told her.

She really respected Bug's transparency. It made her heart happy, seeing him yearn yet strong. She enjoyed to the fullest just being in his arms; before long though they had fallen asleep.

* * *

Serge and Tyra spent all their time on a very strict workout and diet. They both recorded everything they ate for breakfast, lunch, and dinner, and it had to be something that was on the list Serge had made out. Every day after work they worked out, then went for a swim afterwards. Saturday was their day to weigh themselves, check each other's eating plan for the week, and decide if they needed to make any changes.

"You first," Serge gestured to Tyra, as they approached the scale.

"You go," she insisted.

He playfully reached out to grab her, "Girl, get your butt up on that scale."

She was still resisting, so he lifted her and physically put her on the scale.

"Okay," Tyra groaned, not wanting to cause a scene, which is exactly what had happened. They had the attention of everyone in the gym.

Reading the scale, Serge saw she had dropped ten pounds. "Ten pounds!" he exclaimed, loud enough for their newfound audience to hear.

Tyra couldn't help jumping with excitement. When Serge realized how loud he yelled, he tried to duck behind her.

She jumped off the scale, "Okay, your turn."

Serge handed all the papers over to Tyra and stepped up. He had lost two pounds.

"You've been cheating! While I'm eating rice cakes and yogurt, you've been eating cookies and ice cream," she protested.

"I have not been cheating. If you look at my chart, you'll see my goal is to gain muscle, not lose weight. So, I've got to eat a little more. But I still need to watch what I eat. Check out the biceps," he said as he took off his shirt and flexed his muscles for her, "you'll see that I've done just that. I wanna be running around that field like a football player, not a cheerleader. I've got to find my two pounds, though," he said, looking discouraged.

"I'm sorry," she apologized softly, realizing he was very serious.

"Hey, I'm very proud of you," Serge affirmed, changing his mood, and becoming cheerful again. "You really stuck to that diet, didn't you?" he asked her.

"Right down to the water."

"That's good, but I want you to know a lot of that was water weight. Next week you may only lose three or four pounds, which is good. We don't want you to be losing too much in one month. So, we'll stick to this same plan for a while and see how you do. Then we'll decide if we need to change it or not," Serge advised.

"Sounds good. What about you?" she asked him.

"Me, well, I've got to find my two pounds before one of you women find them." Serge smirked, "Just kidding," he added as Tyra gave him one of those serious looks, "I've got to figure out what I can eat more of that won't slow me down, and still give me the weight I need."

"What if you cut out swimming?" she suggested.

"No!" he snapped, "Swimming is good for my breathing and endurance." Serge realized how excited he had gotten, and intentionally calmed himself down. "Plus, it's good for you," he added, trying not to look at her as he said it.

She sensed he really liked swimming, but didn't want to admit it, so she teased him a little longer, "Well, I can swim by myself," she stated.

"No, you can't!" he insisted, getting excited again. Serge laughed at himself, "What I mean is, first off, you're not gonna push yourself. Secondly, we're partners, right? And third, you won't have as much fun without me. I don't know about you, but for me our swim is kind of like our reward for working out so hard."

"Okay, it was just a suggestion. Well, what about the pasta dinners I cook? I could add a little more noodles for you," she offered.

Serge teased her, "You'd do that for me! Are you hitting on me?" With a wink, he added, "No, I'm just kidding. I think that's an excellent idea and I appreciate the offer. What do you say we go out and buy some groceries now?"

"I've got to go to the store anyway," she told him. "If you want, just give me the money and I'll pick up what we need."

Serge pretended his feelings were hurt, "What! You don't want to be seen with me? How about I go with you, so I can at least know what I'm eating, where to find it next time I need it, and you can give me some cooking tips as we stroll the aisles."

"Okay," she agreed, "How 'bout I drive your sports car so I can get used to it, and you can show me all the little things; what to do and what not to do?" Tyra suggested, smiling cunningly at Serge.

They laughed and joked about their bets as they walked out to the car. He was a gentleman still, but he thought about what he wanted, if and when he won the bet, after all the training and challenges.

5

The Unexpected

When they got to the store, Serge took a deep breath, and said a quick prayer to himself before he got out of the car. Tyra just kind of looked at him and got out.

I knew it! Serge said to himself. He had already spotted two of his female friends and they spotted him. He walked close to Tyra, so they wouldn't call him over or make a scene. They respected her, but still made a point of calling his name deliberately, to make it known they knew him. It was nerve provoking, but Serge kept his cool. There were more acquaintances inside and some of the cashiers knew him, also.

Serge and Tyra managed to find all they needed to fulfill the week's menu. He read a lot of the labels. She showed him what she thought was best, too. Everything looked good. He paid for all they gathered, including her purchases. The cashier eyed Serge and Tyra as she rang them up. Tyra couldn't help noticing both their reactions, but she didn't say a thing.

As they headed back to the car, he knew *it* was coming. So, he tried to speak first, "Listen, I know what you're thinking. The truth is I have a lot of female friends, and I admit a lot of them are attracted to me, but that's it."

"Why are you telling me?" she asked. "That's all I am, too. I just thought it was kind of humorous, all the eyes and reactions. All the women speaking at you and calling your name like you're the finest thing walking. No wonder you were saying your little prayer before we went in," she added; mumbling *player* under her breath.

"I heard that!" he responded, before driving off. He looked at her with a serious look, "Tyra, please don't call me that. I'm a salesman. I admit, I try to use all I can to make a lot of my sales, and I do enjoy meeting and talking to people, but I'm no dog or nothing, and that's how you make it sound. I don't go running after every woman I meet. I've had relationships, some have lasted longer than others, but isn't that everybody. I'm sorry if that's the impression I gave you by the way I came off to you. But, that's not the case at all. One day, with the right woman, I'd like to have kids and all that. Okay?" he asked her sincerely.

"Okay," she agreed, softly. Then she touched his hand and apologized.

"So, when are you gonna show me how to cook this pasta?" he asked, changing the subject.

"Well, we don't have time during the week, so how about Sunday evening after church?" she suggested.

"Do you go to church?" he inquired.

"Sure! Don't you?"

"Well, I've been to church," he shared, "but not on a regular basis. What church do you go to?"

"The big red church downtown. We have an excellent men's choir, too," she hinted. "Can you sing?"

"I sing. But I don't know any church songs."

"I bet you do," she mused, as she began to sing, and to his surprise, it was a familiar song.

He joined in and they sang together, jazzing it up, then slowing it back down. Soon they were at her place. Serge helped Tyra take all the groceries inside and looked around her place for a moment. He noticed how neat, clean, and tasteful she kept the place. They agreed to meet Sunday, about three o'clock in the afternoon, and Serge left satisfied.

* * *

All the guys were hanging out at the house. They each shared how they were doing with their New Year's Resolutions. Abruptly, Bug threw a wad of money on the table.

"What's that?" Coop asked.

"Five hundred dollars," Bug told him. "Bunny and I went to the movies the other night."

"Well," Coop said, "Naomi and I are going to church tomorrow. I think you guys do have to get to be friends to a certain extent. I thought our agreement was that we wouldn't get involved by sleeping with these women. You haven't slept with her, have you?" Coop asked Bug.

"No. Honestly, your words keep dancing in my head. Ya know, what you were saying about waiting till marriage."

"Well, that's what God's words are for, to help guide us. I think it would be impossible to be with anyone every day and not feel things. Is she still striving to lose weight? And are you still gonna tryout for the football team?" Coop asked.

"You know I'm still in there," Bug confirmed, getting excited again.

"That's what you were scared of?" K.T. teased him. "He almost fell in love and was trying to fight it," K.T. added full of laughter.

Bug couldn't help laughing, too.

"Well, what's up with you and your girl?" Coop asked K.T.

"Man, I'm straight. That girl is working me out so hard, I don't have time to think of being naughty. She's losing, too. And I know I'm gonna make the team!" K.T. interjected, as he slapped everybody a high five.

"You guys can just push that money right over here. I'm gonna get that jackpot! We're just getting started," Coop provoked.

"Don't get cocky. Let's see how you're doing in about three more weeks," K.T proposed.

"Yeah!" Serge added, "When those hormones start to get backed up, and fighting each other cause they're getting crowded in there and wanna get out."

"Speaking of hormones," Coop said, looking at Serge, "what's up on your end?"

"Man, I'm with K.T. I'm straight. I'm really enjoying these challenges, and I'm curious to see if I can endure to the end. Tyra has finally cut me some slack. So, I feel like I'm accomplishing something. She's doing excellent with her weight. My only thing is I want to gain weight as I work out and build muscle. This week I lost weight. And like I told Tyra, I got to hurry up and find them pounds before some woman finds them," Serge joked. "I can't be running around that field like a little cheerleader; instead of hitting somebody and getting the respect that I deserve they're knocking *me* all around. I wanna go at them the way they're gonna be coming at me, and only the strong will survive."

"Alright," Coop agreed, "that's what I'm talking about! So, when are we gonna get together and practice; help each other out? I want us to all make the team and play together."

"I know, I'm in there," Tipp added, "I'm looking forward to that almost as much as I am me and Gail reaching our personal goals."

"Uh, oh!" K.T. teased, "So, are you thinking about hanging in there for a while?" he asked Tipp.

"Long while!" Tipp confirmed, leaning back with a smile on his face.

"Isn't that ironic," Coop said, "you'd think we've all been waiting around here for some overweight women to settle us down."

"What does that mean?" K.T. asked Coop, "You falling, too?"

"Man, *this* girl is not even the same girl we met at the gym. She's sweet. Yes, she could definitely grow on me," Coop admitted. "She enjoys the studies we do together. She is doing an excellent job with everything we've worked on, and she enjoys a lot of the same things I enjoy. And even if she doesn't slim down, I like the person she is inside, which is really where it counts. But enough about that sentimental stuff. When are we gonna get down to business? We've got to play some! Get right! Get ready!"

"Let's go," K.T. challenged, grabbed the football, and ran for the door. Everybody else ran behind him. K.T. took his position as quarterback, and Bug and Coop squared off against Tipp and Serge. Tipp and Coop on the defense, and Serge and Bug on the offense. They faked each other out, showed each other their moves, and talked about each other the whole time; all in fun.

Some other guys noticed them outside playing around, and they stopped to talk to them, "You guys planning on trying out for the amateur league or something?" they interrupted.

The guys didn't know what to think, "Yeah," Serge spoke up, "what's up?" he asked them.

"Well, me and my boys are planning a little something too," he said pointing at the guys in the car. "You guys interested in a little scrimmage maybe two weeks from now?" the man asked them.

"Yeah," Serge agreed, still not sure about this man they had never seen before, "with or without?" Serge asked.

"With," he answered.

"Without!" Coop interrupted, "We want to play, but we don't want anybody to get hurt messing around."

"Hey!" the man said sternly as he looked at Coop, and threw up his hands, "We're straight man. We're not looking to hurt anyone. We just wanna see where we are and where we need to improve, and at the same time enjoy a little competition. You know tryouts are gonna be with, right?"

"Where are you guys from, anyway?" Coop inquired.

"Up the street," the man answered, "look, my name is Reggie Banks, I'm legit. I've got a wife and two kids. I'm not trying to start any trouble. I just seen you guys hanging out. I figured if you didn't know about the amateur league, I would tell you. Myself, I do plan on being there, and I want us to have the best team. I see my man here with that rocket arm. Hey! I thought you guys might like competition as much as we do, that's all, okay?"

"Yeah, alright," Coop agreed, and shook his hand. "It all sounds good, where do we meet and when?"

"Two weeks from today," Reggie planned, "the park up the street, at four o'clock."

They all looked at each other to make sure everyone was in agreement, then they shook hands with Reggie, and he left.

"Okay, you know what you gotta do," Coop told K.T. "You gotta get those plays right and ready. We all need to be working on our speed and working on those weights." K.T. held out his hand and declared, "All for one, and one for all."

They all piled their hands on top of his and shouted, "One!"

The crew played around a little while longer then called it quits. "I've gotta get showered up. I'm out," Serge said and tossed the football to Coop.

"Yeah, me too," Coop told them, "afternoon service, see ya!" he echoed and tossed the ball to Tipp.

"I've gotta get rolling, too" Tipp added. "See you guys," as he tossed the ball to K.T.

K.T. didn't have any plans, so he tossed the ball to Bug. Bug didn't have any plans either. "Man, I know we're not the only one's sitting around here on Sunday evening with nothing to do," K.T. complained. "Well, I'm gonna ride out to the park. The rules didn't say we couldn't check out the honeys. Are you down?" he asked Bug.

"No, man. I think I'm gonna give Bunny a call and maybe go over to see her. Check out a movie or something," Bug told K.T. as he tossed the ball back.

K.T. stood there for a moment thinking, then he headed to the house. With everybody gone, K.T. changed his mind about being home and decided to ride out to the park. He had a new short set on, fresh cologne, and felt good about himself. He let the top down on his convertible, turned the music up, and leaned back comfortably as he cruised down the road. There was only a hand full of cars at the park, so he left to cruise past a couple of his friends' houses. They weren't home either, so he went by the store and picked up some snacks. While he waited to check out, he scrolled through his phone to see if there were any new movies that interested him for the evening. Then he stopped for some fast food and headed home.

Kicked back on the couch, K.T. planned to hang out by himself. He couldn't help thinking about Gail, and some of the times they had shared together. It made him feel like calling her. But he kept fighting the urge till finally, he gave in. He talked himself into *just* calling her up to make sure everything was still on as scheduled for the week.

Meanwhile, Gail was dealing with the same feelings, trying to keep from calling him. She was home on her couch with a bowl of popcorn. She had thought long and hard about some greasy french fries from her favorite fast-food place, but she didn't give in.

When K.T. called, Gail was really surprised, but glad to hear from him. They were both trying *not* to be too obvious about their excitement and could hardly find words enough to hold a decent conversation. So, after they confirmed their schedule for the week, they said good-bye.

After they hung up, they each knocked themselves for not asking the other about getting together to watch a movie or two. Neither of them wanted to be home alone. Finally, Gail talked herself into asking him. After all, he did call her, now she could call him without feeling too out of place. She still had to play the idea over in her mind a few times before she would have the courage to do it.

K.T. tried to get into the movie he was watching without much success. The phone rang and he picked it up. About to chicken out, Gail started to hang up on him, but she really wanted his company. She asked him real fast if he'd like to come over to watch a movie with her, *if* he wasn't doing anything.

"You know what?" K.T. asked her, "I was just thinking of asking you the same thing. I have the perfect movie in mind."

"Yeah, that would be great. I'll get out the popcorn," she smirked to herself, already settled in with her half-eaten bowl of popcorn.

"Sounds great, I'll be right over," K.T. concealed his excitement. K.T. was still clean and smelling good, but he threw on a little more cologne just to make sure.

Gail ran to the mirror and took a quick peek to see how she looked. Of course, she didn't like what she had on, but she knew just the outfit she wanted to wear. It was great for lounging and looking nice at the same time, plus it made her look slimmer. She threw it on, along with a little perfume, fluffed up her hair, and ran downstairs to put on more popcorn. The doorbell rang. K.T. arrived and was outside the door.

Just as she went to open it, she realized she didn't have any shoes on, and her toenails weren't polished. She tried to hide her feet as she opened the door and acted like she was in a hurry to get to the kitchen. She wanted to find her shoes, so she quickly said, "Welcome, just have a seat anywhere. I'm gonna check on the popcorn."

Unknowingly, K.T. followed her, "I hope you got some butter flavored with extra salt," he said, startling her.

"Oh!" she jumped and turned around, "Here's the salt if you want extra." She didn't have a chance to get her shoes.

They grabbed a bowl for the popcorn and headed back to the living room. They agreed on the movie they wanted to watch and relaxed on the couch. Gail tried to sit in a position to hide her feet, but K.T. noticed, "Why are you trying to hide those feet? You got some ugly feet or something?" he teased. "Let me see them," he insisted.

"You let me see your feet," she fired back.

He snatched his shoe and sock off one foot and showed her his foot. She still refused to show hers.

"Well, you don't mind if I take both my shoes off, do you?" he asked.

"No, get comfortable," she told him, so he did.

Then he snatched the pillow from her feet and grabbed one of her feet. She tried to snatch it back, but she wasn't fast enough. "You got pretty feet," he complimented. "You just didn't want me to see them without that fresh manicure, huh? Let me clean them up," he offered.

"What do you know about doing toes?" she asked.

"I can hook you up. Go get your kit."

Gail laughed, "Eat your popcorn."

"I can eat while I'm doing your toes. Your feet are clean, right?" K.T. asked her.

Gail couldn't help laughing and shaking her head as she headed upstairs for the kit.

As he worked on her toes, she picked up the remote and rewound the movie because they had talked through and missed the first part. But this time they got into the movie.

After a little bit, K.T. hit the pause button on the remote, "Ta-da!" he said as he held up her feet and showed her the job he'd done.

"Wow!" she was astonished, "You want to do my fingernails, too?"

"You, like?" he asked her.

"Yes! You really do know about this stuff, huh?"

"I told you. You think I did good enough to get a drink, though? I really need to wash down some of this salt and these seeds."

"I'm sorry," she jumped up. "I have diet soda, water, and apple juice," she offered.

"Water, please."

Gail fixed them both a tall glass and sat back down to finish the movie.

"Are you always so tense, or is it me?" K.T. asked her.

"I'm relaxed," she told him.

"You are not!" he argued. "You've got to relax! Lean back! Let your hair get messed up! Something! Cause you're making me tense."

"Okay," she agreed.

They both leaned back on the couch, scooting down low in surrender.

"By the way, you look very nice. You smell good too," K.T. teased.

Gail returned the compliment, "You do, too," she said with a giggle. She repositioned the pillow and leaned into it to get even more comfortable. Then K.T. leaned over on her. She smiled and snuggled in more.

They watched two whole movies and talked about them before it got too late, and he had to leave. "Thanks for the evening," K.T. said kissing Gail on the cheek. "I'll see you in the morning," he told her as they walked to the door, and he headed to his car. "Good night!"

When K.T. got home, he just slipped off his shoes and laid back on his bed thinking. "Man! There's no way I could be falling in love," he said to himself. "I know, I've got to stop hanging out with these guys," he reasoned. "Just because they're ready to marry and settle down, doesn't mean I have to," he reached over to set his alarm clock, then drifted off to sleep.

* * *

Over the next couple weeks, they all continued doing their same routines, getting up early, working out, and working out again in the evening. The girls were excelling, and the weight was falling off. They were all proud of themselves as they stepped on the scales. The guys were making progress too, especially Tipp. He was toning and firming up quickly and feeling good.

Bug and Bunny grew closer and closer. Tipp and Elaine began to spend more and more time together, but he was determined to wait for marriage before they could be fully intimate. Serge and Tyra were becoming closer friends. Coop and Naomi grew closer as they studied their Word every morning. The questions she asked him got tougher and tougher, but he loved the challenge. If he didn't know, or couldn't find a Scripture right away, he'd work on it till he did.

6

Ladies' Night

The guys decided to invite all the girls over for dinner. They planned to cook up something special and dress up Saturday night. Then on Sunday they would all meet at the park for a good game of football and fun.

As the ladies drove up in their cars, the guys met them in front of the driveway. Each man performed a different act of hospitality. The ladies were shown where to park; escorted inside; had their coats and purses hung; were served hors d'oeuvres; and club soda in wine glasses of course. Although they weren't drinking alcohol, that didn't stop them from going all out.

Everybody looked great. The table was set. The guys had prepared a nice big salad, steaks, and baked potatoes dressed with chives, placed on a separate dish. Soft music played in the background. They mingled a little until everyone was there then they moved to the dining room for dinner.

Coop stood up first and introduced himself, "I'm David Deveaux, but please call me Coop. I'm so glad everyone could make it. I know you have all kind of met informally, but I'd like to make sure we're all formally introduced. If you don't mind, I'd like to say a prayer to bless the food and this evening first; please bow your heads. 'Father God, we thank You for this gathering of friends, for the food and for Your blessing over this evening. We appreciate all that You give and do for us. We appreciate Your kindness and Your love. And for bringing us together. Please bless the food and the fellowship. We give You thanks and praise, in Jesus' name.'" After the prayer concluded, Coop continued, "I'd like to introduce to you, my date for this evening, Miss Naomi Gayle." Naomi stood with him briefly, waved to everyone, and they both sat down.

Each of the guys stood and introduced themselves and their dates, then they began to eat.

"So, how long have you guys been living together?" Naomi asked Serge.

Serge looked at Coop and raised his eyes as if to say he was impressed by how calm and soft-spoken Naomi was being. "How are you doing, Naomi?" Serge asked in lieu of answering the original question. "Remember me? The one who was on the treadmill 'playing'," he teased.

Naomi laughed, "I do remember I'm so glad we met, and you introduced me to Coop here. Sorry about the treadmill."

"I'm just teasing. Actually, we have lived together since high school, about 8 years. So, if you need to know any of his bad habits, let me know," Serge offered.

They all laughed. "Alright!" Coop jumped in, "What goes around comes around."

They all teased and laughed and told stories and had the girls rolling. After a while, Tipp excused himself to get the dessert, and gestured to Elaine to help him. She followed him to the kitchen, "What can I do?" Elaine asked Tipp.

"Nothing, really. I've just been dying to get a hug and a kiss," he said pulling her into his arms.

Meanwhile, Bug was trying to figure out why Tipp was having Elaine help him when they were supposed to be waiting on the ladies. Bug whispered to K.T., "The ladies aren't supposed to be doing anything."

"Yeah!" K.T. agreed.

They both excused themselves and rushed to the kitchen, "Hey!" they yelled, "Get back in there," they said and carefully grabbed Elaine and gently pushed her out of the kitchen.

"Man, you ain't slick," Bug told Tipp, and slapped him upside the head. "You just gotta wait like the rest of us."

"You guys are fools. You guys obviously didn't see my date," Tipp told them trying to keep his voice down. "Man, she looks good!"

"Sister looking sho' nough good," K.T. agreed. "But did you see Gail?"

They all whispered how nice the ladies looked. Bug jumped in, "Whoa! What about Bunny? Is she hot or what?" Bug got some dap from K.T. then turned to Tipp, "Is she sweet?" and got some more dap.

"Okay!" Tipp responded, and showed excitement, too.

"But check out Naomi," K.T. said. "I believe she came here looking for *that* ring tonight! Coop hasn't moved and has hardly spoken to anyone else," they continued to tease. They laughed so hard and loud, Coop and Serge had to excuse themselves and see what was going on.

"What is going on in here?" Coop asked, leaning his head inside the kitchen door.

K.T. snatched him by the arm into the kitchen, "Man, I think we might have stumbled into something big here!"

"What?" Coop asked looking totally confused.

"Man, did you get a good look at our dates?" Tipp asked.

Coop started to laugh, "Yeah, and do you remember the day we met them?" Bug asked looking at Serge.

"Man, I don't know about you guys, but another couple of weeks might be all I can stand," Tipp confessed. They all laughed and gave each other dap and high-fives in agreement, even Coop.

"Okay, you guys straighten up and let's get back out there. We've been good hosts so far, let's not blow it," Coop said.

They all checked themselves out, straightened up their posture, and headed back to the ladies, as if nothing had happened.

"Where's the dessert?" Tyra asked.

"Oh!" Tipp jumped up, "Guess I got a little side-tracked. Would you mind cleaning off the table guys," he asked, "while I get dessert? Coop, will you get some saucers and clean spoons, too?"

Within a few minutes, they had everything ready. Tipp brought in a big bowl of peach cobbler, "I know what you're thinking. But it's made with all nonfattening ingredients, peaches in their own juice, wheat, honey, cinnamon, and baked slow and on low heat to strengthen the flavor. And for anyone who just doesn't like peach cobbler, I've got something else," he said heading back into the kitchen. Tipp came back out with a tray full of glass bowls filled with sherbet and fruit around the inside of the bowl on top of the sherbet. Both looked so good, the women didn't know which one to have. The men had already decided they were having both.

"Listen, either way, they'll have to be eaten up, so just eat what you want," Tipp told them.

"Okay," they all agreed because they really wanted to try them both.

"Hmm!" Naomi moaned as she tried hers, "Why do I feel so guilty?" she asked.

"Because it's hard to believe something this good could be low cal," Tyra told her, looking at the guys.

Tipp assured them, "Hey, we're all each other's witnesses, all low cal." Everyone agreed, finished their dessert, sat together for a while, and talked.

"We've got one more treat for you ladies, but you have to agree to help us out on this one," Serge told them. "Are you ready?"

"I'm not sure," Bunny looked overwhelmed by everything they had done so far.

"Trust us," Bug told her. "Everything has been nice so far, right?"

"Very!" she assured. "Okay, I'm ready."

They all agreed they were ready, and Serge brought out karaoke. He called Tyra over to him and started the music. He began to sing a familiar duet. She knew the song and was ready when her part came on. He handed her the microphone, and she sang to him. She was really surprised at how good he could sing, but she shocked everybody herself. Tyra's voice was amazing. They both sounded so good together. Everybody gave them a standing ovation when they were finished.

Next was Coop and Naomi's turn. He chose probably the only song he knew which was the theme song to an old popular movie. She didn't really know it, but she listened as he sang it, and joined in when she could. It brought tears to their eyes.

After they finished singing, K.T. got up and teased them, "Now, look what you've done!" he told Coop, handing out tissues. "Naomi, can you give us a song?" he asked.

"I don't know those songs, but I have one I can sing." She complimented Coop on the song he had sung, it was beautiful, then she began to sing, as they cheered. Her voice was also exceedingly beautiful. When she was done, everybody gave another standing ovation.

Tipp and Elaine went next. They chose a duet, too. It had an up-tempo beat, so everybody clapped along as they sang. They added a little dancing as they sang, and everybody gave them their standing ovation, too. Then they handed the microphone over to Serge. He called for Bug and Bunny to go next.

"Hey! God gave each of us different talents," Bunny said trying to get out of singing. "Right, Coop?" she asked.

"Everybody can sing a little," he told her.

"I tell you what, I'll share my talent with you, and if you're not satisfied, I'll try to sing with you, okay?" Bunny proposed.

They all agreed. She went to her purse, took out her little sketch pad, and sat down next to Bug as he began to sing. Bunny sketched them all as a group, and she sketched Bug as he sang. By the end of the song, she was finished. First, she showed it to Bug. It was incredible.

"Ah, man! Bunny! I'm having this," he reacted with enthusiasm. Bug went over to show the others. They all sighed.

"That's not fair, Bug; just because she's your date. We want a copy, too," they all said.

"I can't believe you drew this so fast," Coop added. "Man, what a talent. I guess since everybody is trying to get a copy, you're off the hook."

"Yeah, let her off," Serge agreed, "but we still got one more couple. Okay, K.T. and Gail you're up next."

K.T. played the song he and Gail listened to every day during their work out. It was an oldie, goodie, and they sang it beautifully. After they finished singing, Bug told them to play it over again, as he grabbed Bunny for a dance. The rest of them grabbed their dates and joined in. Everybody sang together, even Bunny, as they danced.

"You have a beautiful voice," Bug whispered in Bunny's ear.

"You think so," she whispered back.

"Yes!" he affirmed.

"Maybe next time I'll try something," she told him.

As the song ended, they all continued to dance, except Coop, "I hate to end this, but I think we better, before it turns out to be a bad date for someone," he whispered to Naomi as he held her in his arms.

"Yeah, I know what you mean," she agreed.

"Okay, fellas!" Coop yelled, "What do you say we get those cars, coats, and purses for the ladies?"

They all stopped dancing and just looked at him for a second.

"Remember our agreement," Coop jarred their memory. When they planned the dinner, they all agreed they would be perfect gentlemen and just have a nice clean evening in every way. They all said their good-byes and saw the ladies off.

7

Growing Pains

After the ladies were gone, the guys all fell on the couch as if they were in agony. "So, how many of you are ready to get married?" Coop asked.

Tipp and Bug raised their hands. A few seconds later Serge put his hand up also.

"Married?" K.T. questioned, "You guys haven't even been dating. You just gonna skip all that so you don't have to feel guilty about having sex with them? What? Do you guys even know what you want in a wife? Do you know what it takes to be a husband? Do you know if your goals and expectations are the same in life? Divorce is just as bad as fornication, you know? I think you guys just want to have some fun, but you better think past the pleasure. There's more to it than that. What happens when the lust wears off, and you're with that person day after day for about a year? All I'm saying is, try to see the whole picture, not just how good it would be to wake up next to a warm body right now. Though, I have to admit, that's a beautiful picture by itself. Reality just doesn't draw pictures quite like that."

"He's right," Coop added, "I know I told you guys about marriage first, and respecting women, but you guys have to be ready to be committed - heart, soul, and body. Ready to make those sacrifices, share everything, especially your money; pick your underwear up off the floor; put the toilet seat down; kiss her and love her even when you don't feel like it; not to mention kids; and giving up a lot of your old ways. It's not always easy. It's gonna be very challenging at times because change doesn't always come easy. Please, pray about it. I would even suggest marriage counseling to just kind of see if you're really ready."

"You mean to tell me, I've gone this far, now you're changing on me?" Tipp asked Coop.

"I'm not changing," Coop said. "Maybe, I just didn't share as much as I should have with you guys. Maybe, I didn't think this through enough. I definitely didn't see all this happening. I don't think anyone has all the answers. I don't want you thinking I do; I stumble just like you. I'm still learning as I go. And some things I have to go through over and over again, before I get a true understanding. But I do know God is real and doing things His way, is the right way, and it's for our good. That's why I've been encouraging you guys as I have. And I'm just continuing to encourage you. First, we were just talking about being friends. Now we're talking about making a lifetime commitment. Anyway, just pray about it, cause it's serious and try to be patient enough to have a plan of some kind; what you both expect, when you want kids, what kind of future you want or hope for. There's a lot to consider." Abruptly ending his speech Coop asked, "Well, what do you guys say we hit this mess and go to bed?"

"What do you say, we just go to bed?" K.T. suggested.

"You know you're the main one who hates bugs," Bug reminded him. "You better come on."

They each started a chore until it was all clean, then headed for bed.

The next morning, Coop got up before everyone else; had his time with God, said special prayers for marriage on behalf of himself and his friends, and was leaving for Sunday School when the others woke up.

The guys had all invited their friends to go with them, except K.T. He felt that was more serious, and he wasn't ready for all that. But he did go to church with them. As it turned out, Gail just happened to visit the same church with a girlfriend of hers. As she listened to the sermon, she looked over and noticed K.T. About the same time, she spotted the others. She tried not to let him see her looking, but realized he had seen her, and she could feel him looking at her. K.T. realized Gail saw all of the other ladies, and now he could feel tension building up, because she wouldn't look at him.

As the preacher closed, Gail whispered to her friend that she had to leave, and she would explain later. When she thought K.T. wouldn't notice, she slipped out. But he did notice, and he slipped out right behind her. He called to her as they got outside, but she kept going. He caught up to her by the time she got to the parking lot.

"What do you want?" she asked him very upset. "I tried to slip out so there wouldn't be any confusion. It's obvious you didn't want me here."

K.T. searched, but couldn't find the words he wanted to say, "Let's go around to the side or to the park or something and talk; not here because it's obvious you're upset."

"I'm upset because I feel humiliated. Everything supposedly went great last night. You put on this great show as if you've got some kind of feelings for me. Then everybody ends up at church, the best part of anything, except me. Isn't that saying enough, K.T.?" she expressed with tears now starting to fall. "What else is there to say?"

"If you give me half a chance, I'll tell you!" he responded, starting to get upset, too.

"Listen," she said calming her voice, "I'll talk to you about this later. I guess I am a little too upset." She tried to walk away, but K.T. stopped her again.

"Please don't leave upset, Gail," he begged her. "You know I like you! That's not the issue! The issue is not what they're all doing. I don't like doing things just because everybody else is doing them. Yes, last night was excellent! But we didn't overstep any boundaries, I hope by sharing a kiss. I kissed you because I do like you. You're starting to grow on me a lot. But there was also a lot of lust along with those emotions, and I don't want it to be about that. When I go to that limit with you, I will be moving toward marriage, and I guess I've always kind of felt the same way about church. The only women I ever saw myself taking to church were my mother and my wife or wife to be. Listen, I told you before, I don't want anyone to get hurt. But before I commit or allow this friendship to become a serious relationship, I've got to feel I'm ready. Aren't you gonna do the same? I know you've broken a few hearts," he said, hoping to get a smile. "Had a few of those *friends* fall in love with you, only to find you weren't ready for the things they were ready for. Didn't you want to be sure and not just move because people expected you to?"

Finally, she calmed down, "I'm sorry. I guess I was just feeling left out, and my self-esteem was stepped on. But I understand, and I agree totally. Plus, I know you had no way of knowing I'd be at this church." She gave him a hug, and he squeezed her extra tight.

"Thanks so much. I don't want to lose my new friend," he said as he held her. "Are you still gonna hang out with us for football?" he asked her as he released her and made eye contact.

"Yeah. I'll see you guys after I go home and change."

He held her hands for a second, and he apologized, "I'm sorry. I really didn't intend or even think that I was gonna hurt you. Are you okay? Are we okay?"

"Yes," she said, smiled, got into her car, and headed off.

Finally, church was over. Coop had seen everything from where he was sitting and rushed out to see if everything was alright, "Are you good?"

"Yeah," K.T. said and breathed a sigh of relief. "Man, I'm sure glad you taught me about honesty. And I think being in the right place helped, too," he said looking up at the sky, with a silent thank you to Jesus.

They all gathered in the parking lot, chatted for a few minutes, and went to their own houses to change. Shortly after, they met back up at the park.

As they were throwing the ball around, they came up with rules for today's game. Everyone was there, except for Gail. K.T. started to get a little worried. Then he spotted her driving up. Distracted, focused on Gail, K.T. got hit upside the head with the ball. K.T. brushed it off and ran over to her car.

"How do you feel?" he asked her.

"Still kind of goofy," she admitted, walking slowly.

"Well," he picked her up onto his shoulders and started to run, "let's see if this will help."

Gail broke out in laughter. She screamed until he put her down. And it definitely helped.

8

Let's Play

Coop started as they all gathered around, "Okay, since I hear Gail is such a good quarterback, if she doesn't mind, we're gonna have her quarterback against K.T. The rest of us will split up. Serge, Tyra, Tipp, and Elaine will go with K.T. against me, Naomi, Bug, and Bunny with Gail. We're gonna flip to see who gets the ball first." Coop pointed out the touchdowns for both sides. "We're just playing touch, nobody gets too aggressive, alright? Does anybody want to add anything?" he asked.

They all yelled a collective, "No!"

"Okay, then. Team 1, call it in the air," Coop instructed as he flipped the coin.

"Heads," K.T. called out.

Coop let it hit the ground, and it was heads.

"That was just luck," Gail sassed. "Sooner or later luck runs out."

"I guess, it's gonna be later," K.T. teased, "so don't take this loss personally, okay?"

K.T. called his team to a huddle, "They're gonna be looking for a slow start, but I'm going straight for the bomb. Tyra, you and Serge are going as far as you can, on the count of ten, turn and look for the ball wherever you are. Elaine, you go out just a little, and be ready in case I have to release it sooner. And Tipp, you stay and block for me. Men on the right, ladies on the left, hut!" K.T. hit the ball and they took their places.

Tipp hiked the ball, and they all ran out. Gail tried to touch him, but he was too fast for her, while Tipp kept Coop out of the way.

Soon K.T. let it go as hard as he could throw. Serge and Bug both jumped for it. Serge got it and they scored. They chanted and yelled for a few seconds as they set up to throw the ball to the others.

When they received the ball, Gail said, "I'll run it. I want to see what those women got."

Tyra had some speed. They tried to block her, but she got passed them. She caught up to Gail and touched her. K.T. looked at Gail and smiled. She smiled back and set the ball down where she got caught.

Gail called her team into the huddle, "Well, we see these girls aren't too sloppy, so let's try something new. I'm gonna drop back as if to throw long. Coop, you stay just behind me. I'm going to toss the ball to you then run behind you. You pass it back to me and I'm going to hit Bug or Bunny long, or Tyra short. Everybody try to stay on the inside of whoever is guarding you because I don't have the arm that K.T. has." They clapped their hands and assumed their places.

Her team ran it just like she said. When Coop passed the ball back to Gail, he blocked for her. She put it right in Bug's hand and he ran it in for the touchdown. They all had their victory celebration, as well.

They ran a few more plays, and both scored another touchdown. The women started to get tired and agreed to sit on the sidelines and watch while the men continued to play.

After a few minutes they noticed a group of guys approaching them. Not knowing what was going on, the women stood to their feet to get the guys' attention. They looked at the women, then noticed the men who were approaching.

"Hey, what are you guys doing here?" K.T. asked.

"What's up, man?" Reggie said and slapped him some dap. "We just saw you guys over here. Saw the girls playing, too. That one's got a pretty good arm," he said with a smile and pointed at Gail.

"Yeah, excellent," K.T. agreed. "So, have you guys signed up yet? The fifteenth is the deadline, right?"

"Paid up and ready to play," Reggie told him with confidence.

"So, what's up, you guys wanna run a little bit?" Bug asked.

"I thought you'd never ask," Tony, one of the other guys with Reggie said going out for a pass.

K.T. shot the ball to him, and it hit him right in the chest.

They each took sides. Reggie, of course, was the quarterback for his team. He drew back to throw, and Coop stopped him. He remembered they just left the girls on the sidelines.

"Hold up," Coop hollered to Reggie, then turned to talk to his guys, "Listen, I'm gonna ask the women if they don't mind going to pick up the food and a few blankets so we can eat here at the park. We can run a game till they come back."

All went as planned. The women didn't mind and they all rode with Gail, who got the keys from Coop, and instructions of where to find everything.

"So, what do you ladies think about these men we've become friends with over the past couple months?" Gail asked them as they drove away.

Bunny answered first, "It's scary. Meeting them the way we did; having someone help us reach our goals, feeling good, love, enjoyable times, and no sex!"

"I think we can all thank Coop for that," Elaine added. "He's always trying to instill worthwhile qualities and values into them. And I know it has made a difference for me and Tipp."

"For me, too," Naomi added in. "He's special. I'm so thankful I met him. And it is kind of scary. It's like being caught up in a good dream. I'm losing weight, feeling good about myself. I'm happy; starting to feel like I'm in love. I have hopes and dreams. I've got God in my life, plus me and Coop get along great," Naomi smiled and closed her eyes as if dreaming.

"That's great," Gail showed her support. "I can't say the same. K.T. *says* he really likes me, but it seems we're always trying to wait on 'the man' to get ready to fall in love with us. Sometimes, I just get so frustrated with that; especially when I find myself fighting to keep my feelings under control. All I was planning to do was get myself together. Then, here he comes with his fine butt, all up in my face. Now, he's got my heart all tangled up, and he don't know what to do with it."

"I know what you're saying girl," Tyra related. "But I'm glad Serge did pursue. Cause I've tried over and over again to really stick to a diet and workout plan and couldn't. Now, it doesn't even feel like I'm struggling. I'm actually enjoying myself. But I gave him such a hard time initially. If he hadn't pursued me the way he did, my heart would have probably grown even more bitter. It wasn't that I couldn't stand men, it was more like I couldn't stand the risk of anymore rejection. I wasn't going to even expect or ask for anything from any man. But girl, you just hang in there. K.T. might be fooling you. I can read a man like a book. That man ain't no fool. He knows a good thing when he sees one. And you do have to give them men a little while to get through that old tough outer fear. He cares. That's why he busted up out the church the way he did today. What happened, anyway?" Tyra asked.

Gail laughed, "To tell you the truth, we just really had no way of knowing each other would be at that church, and I guess I felt left out, cause all of you were invited. But after we talked, I did understand he just takes going to church with someone more serious. And as it stands right now, we're just not where you guys are, and I'm not sure if we will be."

"You just hang in there," they all encouraged her.

"Now, we've got to do something special for them," Bunny suggested. "Last night was too good. We've got to show them we know how to go all out, too."

They all agreed.

"What do you say we get together at my place this Friday night and make plans?" Gail offered.

"Sounds good. Everybody bring some ideas. We're gonna have to stand them up without letting them know what we're doing," Elaine added.

They exchanged phone numbers, got the food and blankets, loaded the car, and headed back to the park.

Meanwhile, the guys were having a blast. They were beating the other men by two touchdowns. When they spotted the women, they decided to end the game.

"Okay guys, all or nothing," Coop said. "If we make this touchdown we win; if we don't, you win."

"Alright," everybody agreed.

"How's that arm feeling?" Coop asked K.T in the huddle.

"I don't know man. I think we might want to go for the speed on this one," K.T. answered honestly.

"How do you feel, Serge?" Coop asked.

"I'm in there," Serge confirmed. "He ain't got nothing. But we've got to all go different ways so once I do beat him, no one else will have a chance."

"Alright," K.T. directed the play, "Serge, left. Bug, right. Coop, short. Tipp, low to block."

They all clapped and set up. Serge and Bug took off strong crossing over before they got too far from K.T. As planned, K.T. put the ball right in Serge's hand and he was gone for the touchdown. The ladies got there just in time to cheer them on.

"Good game guys," they said to their opponents and shook hands.

"Next week, we're gonna bring our fans, too," Reggie added. "We'll see you guys next week. Same place." They all shook hands. Reggie and his group left them to have lunch with the ladies.

9

Expecting the Unexpected

"I take it you guys won," Naomi proudly asked the guys.

"Yeah," Coop said. "I don't know why, but I keep getting a funny feeling when I'm around this Reggie guy. It seems like he just wants to have fun and play, so I'm trying not to make anything of it, but that feeling won't go away."

"Don't worry about it," Bug told him. "Check him out if you feel you need to. Find out where he lives, works, who he hangs out with, whatever, but don't worry about it."

"I can get you that information at my job," Gail offered. "What's his name?"

"Reggie Banks," Coop answered.

"Alright then," K.T. interrupted, "let's eat."

They all ate till they were stuffed, then headed for the blankets.

"Hey, where are the pillows?" Bug yelled. being sarcastic.

"I got mine right here," Tipp said, as he laid his head on Elaine, "and I'm not sharing. You guys have to get your own."

"Oh, is that how they're making them now? This one must be mine then," Bug said and laid his head on Bunny.

"Yeah," Tipp confirmed with ease, like it was a perfect fit, "this one is mine."

Serge joined in, "How do you know?" he playfully asked while he patted Tyra, as if he was testing a pillow to see if it was his. "Oh, yeah! This is mine right here?"

Coop looked at Naomi. "And I'm yours," Naomi confirmed and pulled Coop's head into her arms. He just laughed and fell into rhythm.

Gail didn't give K.T. a chance to say anything. She felt awkward, so she stood up, and instead asked K.T. if he wanted to go for a walk.

"No! I want my pillow," K.T. teased trying to get her to loosen up.

She tried to smile, but not much came of it. She just looked at him and waited for him to get up. He got up and they headed further into the park.

"Awkward, huh?" K.T. asked Gail, as they walked off.

"Yeah," she said, "I don't know if I can do this group thing anymore. Not with them all being so close, and us well," she paused. "If you still want to work out in the morning that's fine."

"What about the afternoon?" he asked her.

"I want to keep working out, but I think we're spending way too much time together," she expressed. "I've got to cut back. My feelings for you have grown too much as it is. I'm starting to develop some angry feelings inside, and I don't like it. I feel like I have to wait for you to feel the same way about me and the truth is, it may never come to that. And I just can't see always waiting for the man to decide if I'm good enough, or whatever."

"Look, Gail," K.T. interrupted, "it's not a matter of whether or not you're good enough, pretty enough, or whatever. It's knowing whether we're really compatible, whether we're going in the same direction and can make it last, and then deciding that's really what we *both* want to do. Just like you've been hurt, I've been hurt, too. It's not always the man doing the walking out. I know you feel like you're ready for a relationship, and all that, but how well do you know me, Gail? You don't even know any of my bad habits yet and if you can tolerate them! I told you; I really like you. Why can't we just relax and continue enjoying and getting to know each other for now. If you want, we can even go steady. I won't date anyone but you."

"If I want!" she repeated. "Listen, it's obvious you're not ready for anything, so all I'm saying is let's back off some of the time we're spending together, and some of these romantic episodes, so hanging out and being friends will be easier."

He wrapped his arms around her and held her close to him, "I care, Gail. But I'm not like everyone else."

"I'm not holding that against you. I'm just trying to keep my heart intact, just as you are."

"Why, Gail? I don't understand."

"What don't you understand?" she asked him.

"I don't understand why we can't just date for now."

"Because," she wept, "I'm ready for so much more and you don't feel the same and it hurts and it's hindering me. I have to act a certain way, control my every feeling and my thoughts. I can't do that all the time," she told him.

He continued to just hold her tight, his face against hers, as they both kept silent for a moment. K.T. abruptly made a proposal, "Marry me then."

"That's not fair K.T.," Gail dropped her arms in frustration.

He pulled her away from him so he could look into her face, "I'm serious. Marry me and promise you'll never leave me."

"I can't," uttered Gail.

"Why, Gail?"

"Because, you're just saying something in the moment. Can you look into my eyes and tell me you love me with all your heart; the way a husband loves a wife; the way someone would who wanted to spend the rest of their life together?"

Overwhelmed by Gail's response, K.T. dropped his head on her shoulder, "Talk about not fair. Do you love me?" he asked her.

"Yes! I do," admitted Gail.

"How?" K.T. pondered, "Love takes time to grow. It doesn't just happen like that. Love at first sight. Do you believe in that?"

"Yes, I do. But this isn't first sight, right?"

"It's weak though," reasoned K.T, "because you're already giving up and walking away. That's exactly what I'm talking about. Once I put that ring on your finger, I don't want you to walk out because you're mad or frustrated, disappointed, or whatever. Can't you see I care, Gail?

Frustrated, Gail asked, "Why is love so complicated?"

"Why? Because it's special, but delicate and has to be handled with extreme care. What if we agreed to get engaged to be married when we reach our goal? That way we can spend as much time as we want together, and our love can have a chance to grow and get stronger and we can each have time to really think about everything."

She smiled and wiped the tears from her eyes, "Yeah?" she asked, seeking reassurance.

K.T.'s smile brightened up both of their faces. He dropped to one knee. He took the ring he wore on his finger and held it in his hand, grabbed her hand, and asked, "Would you wait a little longer for me, Gail?"

"Yes," committed Gail. She sat on his knee, received the oversized ring, and gave him a big kiss.

Bug spotted K.T. on one knee and alerted everyone, "Yo, look!" Once Bug had their attention, he pointed to Gail and K.T.

"What is he doing?" asked Coop.

"He's either begging or bugging," Serge reasoned.

Tipp chimed in, "I know that's not my boy over there on one knee, Mr. I'm not gonna rush."

"You don't never know when it's your time," Coop quietly interjected.

"And most of the time, it's not when you think it is. But good gracious! I didn't think my boy would go out like that," Serge said.

Coop added, "He must have been in some serious denial. He's obviously been feeling more than he led us to believe. Sounds like somebody else I know," Coop looked at Bug.

Bug winked at him and smiled, then he looked at Bunny, tucked under his arm.

When they saw K.T. stand up, they all jumped back down on their blankets. "Here they come!" alerted Tipp. They all tried to act like they didn't see anything.

K.T. and Gail rejoined the group, "We've got some news to share with you all," K.T. said, eager for everyone's attention. As they sat up, K.T. noticed they all had genuine smiles on their faces. "What's everyone smiling about?" K.T. couldn't help but ask.

"Oh nothing," they lied, while trying to wipe the smiles from their faces.

K.T. formally made the announcement, "Well, Gail and I are considering marriage. Nothing official yet, but it's our goal."

"What!" Bug jumped to his feet and touched K.T.'s forehead with his palm, to check to see if he felt alright, teasingly.

"Okay," K.T. said, "go ahead, tease me. I deserve it."

Bug hugged him and acted like he was weeping, "I'm gonna miss you man."

K.T. joined in and acted like he was crying along with Bug, "I'm gonna miss all you guys, too," he said, as he went around and hugged them all. The ladies all hugged Gail.

Gail explained their plan, "K.T. said we're going to get passed all the challenges we've set. Then we agreed to make a decision at that time."

"Excellent choice," the guys agreed.

Tipp winked his eye to let K.T. know he stood with him, "What do you say we pack up and go back to the house for a little celebration. Play some games, maybe watch a movie."

"Yeah!" Elaine shouted, "The ladies against the guys."

All in agreement, they shook off the blankets, packed up their things, and headed back to the house.

Each couple rode in separate cars. Coop and Naomi drove back to the house quietly. Naomi looked out the window and slightly envied the fun she saw the other couples having. As they passed by, she heard their radios blare the same upbeat song, while they sang along and goofed around. When they arrived at the house, Naomi sat in the car for a minute and looked intently at Coop.

"What's wrong?" he asked her.

"Do you ever listen to the radio, Coop?"

"Yeah, mostly though when someone else has it on. Not that I don't care for music, I just try to take advantage of opportunities like that to be fed and grow spiritually. You know what I mean?"

"Yeah," she responded, softly staring up into the clouds.

"Does that bother you, Naomi?"

"No, I like listening to gospel music. It feeds me, too."

"There's something on your mind, though. What is it?" Coop looked sincerely into her face.

"Alright," she adjusted herself, "I'm gonna try to say this without sounding silly."

"You know me, I don't take anything you say as silly," he told her.

Naomi paused for a minute then she started, "I know how you feel about premarital sex, and I'm in agreement. My body doesn't always agree, but my spirit agrees. But do you realize we've never even shared an intimate kiss? Is that forbidden, too?"

"Actually, it is," Coop explained, "because of how it stirs up our other hormones. Why? Are your lips longing like mine?" he teased.

"That's not funny, Coop! You're making fun of me."

"No, I'm not," he said, as they joked around. "The truth is, I'm a Christian, but I'm very much human, too. This flesh gets out of control enough on its own. Now, say we start necking and squeezing and caressing and all that. Are you gonna stop? I can't promise you that I will. And I know me, I'll be feeling too guilty after I allow myself to go too far. I know, you have needs just like me. And yes, the Bible says it's better to marry than to burn. So, what do you say we do the right thing, too?" he asked her.

"What?" she tried not to get too excited or scream or cry.

"Let's consider getting *that* counseling, too."

"Coop!" Naomi finally let go and screamed. "Are you sure?"

"If you say yes," he told her.

"Oh, Coop," she whispered, then shouted, "yes!"

He kissed her softly on the lips and they went inside. Naomi tried to keep from blushing but couldn't.

Coop was happy, too, especially because he knew how excited she was. They went inside and approached the rest of the gang.

Coop spoke first, "Well guys, we've got more good news to share."

"What?" Bug looked as if he was gonna start up again. "Not you, too?" he pretended to start crying.

"Yes, us, too," Coop responded. "We're going to get *that* counseling started, as well. That is if K.T. and Gail don't mind sharing."

K.T. slapped him some dap and gave him a big hug. Then once again they all shared a group hug and pretended to cry.

"I'm gonna miss you guys," Coop shared.

All the women hugged Naomi and their tears were real. They sobbed, "It's so beautiful."

"Okay, guys," Serge interrupted. "Cut that stuff out, now! Come on, now! What's wrong with you people? This should be a time of rejoicing."

"Yeah, let's have a toast. I'll get the glasses and the grape drink," Bug joked.

"I'll help you," Bunny followed him into the kitchen.

Bug noticed Bunny was unusually very quiet, "Oh, don't you get crazy on me, too."

"What's that supposed to mean?" Bunny asked him.

"I don't know," he stopped everything he was doing.

"Do you think I want to get married?"

"Yes, I do," replied Bug. "And why are you looking so sad all of the sudden?"

Bunny attempted to keep their conversation from going in that direction, "Look, June, we don't want to have this discussion right now. Let's just let them enjoy their time, okay?"

"Okay," Bug agreed, grabbed the glasses, and headed for the door. He intentionally stopped at the door, making her bump into him.

"What are you stopping for?"

"Because I don't feel right," Bug pulled her back into the kitchen.

"Listen Bug, I'm not envious or jealous that Naomi and Gail are engaged. I'm happy for them. When it's our time, it'll happen, okay?" she tried to change to a happier tune. "Don't worry and please don't feel obligated. If I seem moved, I am. I guess women go through more stages; they laugh, they cry, they reminisce. But I'm fine," Bunny kissed Bug on the cheek.

"Let's go then," he said, "before they have to come looking for us."

Bug and Bunny put all the glasses on the table, filled them, and passed them out to everyone.

"Here's to love, peace, and happiness for all," Coop raised his glass and gave the first toast. They all raised their glasses in agreement.

K.T. tipped his glass, "Here's to friends, family, loved ones, hopes, dreams, and a future of success and fulfillment."

Tipp gave his toast next, "Here's to marriage and babies and growing old together. Sharing, giving, and a commitment of love and happiness."

"Here's to two becoming as one, in every way, and no matter what it takes, keeping the love alive," Bug toasted.

Serge chimed in, "Here's to love always just as it is today and even greater."

"Here's to romance, honeymoons, cuddling on warm nights and waking up to loving arms," Gail added, getting a sigh and a hug from K.T.

"Here's to God, who knows and meets all our needs, and uses special people like each of you to make dreams come true," Naomi shed a tear.

"Here's to the best of everything which is what you guys deserve. Let nothing and no one separate what is brought together in holy matrimony," Bunny added with cheer.

"Here's to friends, first and always, someone to always be there, to always care, to help, to comfort, to lean on, to hold, to love, to make life happier, and enjoyable in every way," Elaine lifted her glass.

"And here's to knowing what it takes to have a good, loving, neverending, happy, fulfilling, and all that you want it to be, marriage," Tyra finished off.

"See, you guys have gotten all in the romantic mood and everything, we're supposed to be playing the game we set up. Men against women, not with the women." Coop yelled, breaking everything up, "Let's go! Get away from them before they mess up your heads." It worked; Coop managed to break up all the cuddling that was going on by the time they all finished their toasts.

The competition was on. They had a big sketch pad, a stand, and everything needed. Each couple took turns being judges. They played till it was almost time for bed. Everyone was so exhausted; all they could do was say good night and head home. Still, by the time they each climbed into their own beds, their minds wandered, as they looked at the ceiling. Eventually, sleep prevailed.

* * *

They were all starting to get burnt out with their intense exercise regimen. Especially, early mornings. But they looked forward to seeing each other even more than getting in shape. That's what kept them motivated and going.

Monday morning, Bunny checked on Mr. Reggie Banks to see what she could find. She saw that he was employed at the Amateur All American Football League and more surprisingly, he was the head manager. She rushed to call Elaine as soon as she found out to get her input, "What am I gonna do? I can't tell the guys."

"Just tell them you checked him out, and he appeared to have a good honest record – a job and everything."

"But what if they ask me where he works?" Bunny thought of all the 'what ifs'.

"Stall them, tell them you'll get it to them later," advised Elaine.

"Well, I've got to tell the others so they can keep the guys from checking up on Reggie for themselves," cautioned Bunny.

"I just know they'll be all nervous and everything if they find out. They probably wouldn't even be able to play right. Then again, it might be encouraging for them to know who the man is checking them out," Elaine went back and forth with it.

"We'll see what the others say," Bunny decided.

She called each of the other ladies. They all unanimously agreed *not* to say anything unless they asked, specifically. And if they did ask, they would be given as little information as possible without lying. As it turned out, the guys seemed to have forgotten all about it throughout the week.

Next, they had to figure out how they were going to get away Friday to get their little act together. Naomi told Coop she had some papers to sort that evening; Gail told K.T. she had to do a little shopping, even invited him to come, knowing he'd say no; Bunny and Elaine said they were gonna get together and hang out for a little while and told the guys they'd catch up with them later in the evening; and Tyra told Serge she planned to hang out with some friends, and asked him if they could have breakfast the next morning, so he was content.

Friday night came and they all met at Gail's place with their ideas and were excited about it. Gail suggested they sing a song together dedicated to the men. They all liked the same kind of music, so they quickly agreed on the perfect song. They rehearsed and since everybody knew the song, and they all could sing, it only took two practices, and it sounded good; especially considering they didn't have any music. Tyra knew the owner of a poetry and singer's club she used to go to, and she thought it would add an extra special touch if, somehow, they could perform for them on stage. They all agreed, so she planned to call and talk to the owner as soon as she could. Naomi came up with the idea to give them all football shirts alike with their names on the back. They each had to find out what their guy's old numbers were so they could have them put on the shirts, also. They decided on the clothes they would wear, the foods they would have, and they were done.

* * *

The guys thought it was a little peculiar, all the ladies stood them up that night. Bug was the first to mention it, "They are up to something. It's no coincidence. I'll bet if we ride to one of their houses, we'll find all of them," he said convincingly.

"Hey! That's enough," Coop said.

Serge held up the keys to the car and asked Coop, "Well, don't you want to know, too?"

Coop was speechless. He couldn't resist. He grabbed the keys, and they all ran to the car.

The ladies had just left Gail's house when the guys came from the opposite direction and missed them. They drove by each of their houses, but they each made it home before the drive by.

Bunny and Elaine tried to reach Bug and Tipp on their house phone. It rang and rang. They were certain someone would be home, so they called again and left messages. Finally, the guys returned home.

"Now, don't you feel guilty?" Coop asked them.

"I sure do," Bug said, but I'm still not convinced.

Each one of the guys slapped him upside the head and went into the house. They checked their messages and realized the ladies had tried to call them numerous times. They brainstormed possible excuses to use to explain why they weren't home.

"Hey! I got it!" Tipp hollered. "We went riding. It's the truth, right?" he said, looking at Coop.

"It's part of the truth. But it's not a lie," Coop said. They all cheered up.

Serge added, "Just hope they don't ask for more information than that."

They ended the night with telephone calls to the ladies and called it a night.

* * *

By the next day, the ladies had confirmation from the owner of the poetry and singer's club. They had another conversation to finalize the details among themselves. Then they were able to get the guys to agree to the ladies doing a little something special for them since they had treated them so royally on their night.

10

Ladies' Turn

Before they knew it, *their* night had come. They dressed in their finest. Everybody looked like someone from a magazine. They all decided to go back to Gail's after the date and spend the rest of the evening at her house; including eating the dinner they had prepared. Each one of them had left work a little early to make sure everything was ready. The ladies agreed to pick up the men.

Once they got to the club, the ladies made sure they got a seat right in front of the stage. There was another group on stage performing when they got there. As they finished, the ladies excused themselves to go to the ladies' room. Instead, they snuck around to the stage. The owner of the club introduced them as special guests, and they entered the stage. They made their entrance, and the guys couldn't believe it. They smiled and leaned back in their chairs, as the ladies began to sing. By the end of the song, each of the men had a serious look on their face.

They couldn't believe how good their ladies sounded. Even the manager was astounded. Everyone in the crowd stood, clapped, and whistled, especially the guys. An encore was requested, but they didn't dare, knowing they only rehearsed one song.

Each lady walked into the arms of her man and was received with a great big hug.

"You guys were beautiful," Coop started to say but before he could finish, the manager came over to their table.

"Gail, you didn't tell me you guys were gonna tear up the place," the manager boasted. "I came to say thank you, and to see if you ladies might be interested in coming back on a regular basis. Don't give me an answer tonight," he interjected before they had a chance to comment, "just think about it."

After they watched a few more acts, they headed to Gail's house. A fully prepared meal greeted them, which consisted of stuffed peppers, baked chicken sautéed in mushroom sauce, pasta salad, a tray of shrimp with cocktail sauce, and cheese sticks. For dessert they had fruit sticks with just about every kind of fruit you can think of on them, a lemon moraine pie, and homemade fruit filled gelatin topped with whipped cream. Everybody ate till they were ready for a nap, but the girls had one more surprise for them.

They relaxed in the living room and their surprises were brought to them. Each was handed a box and told to open it. As soon as they realized what they received, their energy was renewed. They jumped to their feet and started yelling.

"Yes! We're a team again!" Bug yelled.

"Oh, you ladies are the best!" Coop told them.

Big hugs were given and received, as the cheer continued. Bunny hadn't thought about Reggie anymore until that moment. And when she did, she tried to ease away before anybody else thought about him. She asked the ladies to help her clear the table, while the guys talked about what great shape, they felt they were in, and how great everything was gonna go.

After a few minutes, they heard soft music playing in the background. The ladies returned to the room and were welcomed by the extended hand of their man for a dance. They only danced one dance and decided that was all they could take.

The ladies had to take the men home because they picked them up. Each couple made an extra stop on their way home, except Coop and Naomi.

Tyra and Serge went for a quick drive by the beach. Bug and Bunny stopped by the gym where they first met and had a few laughs as they talked about all they had been through. K.T. and Gail drove by the park where they had spent so much of their time. Tipp and Elaine reminisced at a spot on the beach where they used to go and just sat in the car, listened to music, watched the moon, and wrapped up in each other's arms.

Coop and Naomi ended up cuddled together outside and watched the moon as they waited for everyone else to arrive. Soon everyone arrived, and they all called it a night.

* * *

They all got together again during the week. While at dinner, Bug posed the question to the group, "Why are we *not* having bachelor and bachelorette parties, instead of everybody together?"

"Because it's not time for that yet," Bunny nicely told him.

"Yeah, what's wrong with that?" Tyra asked.

Ready for dinner, K.T. changed the subject, "Can we eat? Man, that food smells good!"

"Sure," Tyra said as her and the rest of the women arranged the food on the table. Everybody ate till they couldn't eat anymore.

11

Gifts for All

They had all gotten gifts for the couples who were going through marriage counseling.

"Okay," Serge hopped up to grab his gift bags, "open my gifts first." He handed one to Naomi, and one to Gail.

Naomi opened hers, and it was a baby car seat. Everybody started laughing.

"A car seat?" Naomi asked.

"Yep," Serge was confident, "if you know Coop like I know Coop, you're gonna need that real soon. That man been waiting on a wife for about seven years."

They all laughed even harder. Gail blushed, "I'm afraid to open mine."

"Go ahead, it's all good," Serge assured. It was a large ice chest. "Open it up," he directed Gail. She opened it and inside was a tent.

"Alright!" K.T. said.

"Yeah," Serge explained, "I know my man here likes to camp out, and I see you like that morning sunrise, so you guys can camp out and watch the sunrise all in one."

"Thanks," K.T. told him, as he gave him a hug.

"Yeah, thanks," Naomi added giving him a hug, too.

"Alright! Enough of that mushy stuff," Bug interrupted. "It's too early for that." He went over and got his gifts from the table. He handed one small box to each of them. They all opened them at the same time. Inside were nice watches. As they examined them a little closer and admired them, they found their names and the date they met in the center. They were speechless.

"Thanks, my man. I won't ever be able to forget our anniversary date with this," K.T. showed his appreciation.

"Sho', you right," Bug said as they exchanged hugs. The ladies hugged him and thanked him, too.

Last was Coop, "Thanks, man. That's very nice." He hugged him and sat down.

"Okay, I guess I'm next," Tyra grabbed her boxes and handed them each to the ladies.

Naomi passed hers to Coop, "Here your turn."

"Well, thank you," Coop said and opened it up. Inside was a very nice short set for Coop and a matching dress for Naomi, both made from matching flowered Hawaiian material. Underneath the clothes was an envelope. Coop opened it and it contained two tickets for a cruise to Jamaica. Naomi screamed and hugged Coop, then jumped up and hugged Tyra.

"Yes! Thank you," Coop jumped up to give Tyra a hug, also.

Gail allowed K.T. to open theirs. They had matching warmups with an envelope, too. They opened it and discovered a ski trip to Colorado.

"Yes!" they both shouted.

"Man, you guys got some good taste," K.T. complimented.

"Well, what do you say we add some romance to this evening?" Bunny grabbed her gifts. She handed one box to each of them. They opened them all. The ladies held up sexy, silk sleepers, with matching jackets. The men showed off their sexy silk boxers with matching jackets.

Everybody *ooh'ed* and *ah'ed*, as they touched them. K.T. slapped their hands away, "Hey! Nobody be touching this but me," he told them as he took Gail's gown and put it back in the box.

"I know that's right," Naomi agreed and took Coop's boxers, giving him a sexy look. "For my hands only," she put them back in the box.

They all thanked Bunny and gave her a hug.

Next, Elaine got up to give her gifts. She gave them each a box to open together. Inside both of them was a statue of a black bride and groom which signified them, engraved with their names. They were indescribably beautiful. She knew the women would be overwhelmed, but the men were moved just as much. They hugged Elaine and thanked her, too.

Tipp picked up his gifts and handed them out. They each opened them and found a big plaque titled, *What Marriage Means*. Beneath the title, was a list of things to remind them what their marriage means. They were lovely and heartfelt.

"Man, I didn't know you had it in you," K.T. told Tipp, then they each gave him a hug.

"Okay," Coop said, "I have a gift for you guys." He grabbed it from the table and gave it to them. Gail opened hers and found a couple of books titled, *How to Keep Love Alive,* and a very nice Study Bible.

"Thanks, Coop," Gail shed tears and hugged Coop.

"You're a special person," K.T. hugged him, too.

Coop had one more box. He handed it to Naomi, "These belonged to my mother, and I want you to have them."

She opened the box and inside was an elegant pearl necklace and earring set. Naomi was overwhelmed at how breathtaking they were, "Oh Coop! Oh God! Thank you!" She was nearly speechless, and hugged Coop, till they had to pull them apart.

"Okay, guys!" Naomi jumped up to find her gifts in the bunch, "My turn." She handed one box to Gail, another to K.T., then a bigger box to Coop and told him to wait for Gail and K.T. to open theirs first. They opened their box and found matching African outfits. The head pieces were embroidered. One said king, and the other queen. They were unique and stunning. Finally, Coop opened his box. Laid smoothly in the box was a very nice, double-breasted suit and a gold chain with a charm. The charm was half of a cross. Naomi gestured to draw attention to the matching chain on her neck, with the other half of the cross on it. They both had the same sentimental statement engraved on them: *We'll bear our cross together.* Coop put his around his neck and gave Naomi a tearful, thanks, and held her in his arms.

"I've got one for you guys, too," K.T. handed the box to Coop, as Naomi continued wiping tears from her eyes. He opened it. There were a set of matching champagne glasses with their names written on them. Also in the box, was a bottle of grape juice and crackers. Coop laughed as he pictured the humor of the grape juice and crackers for communion. Naomi was not familiar with communion, so she didn't get it. She looked at Coop and waited for him to stop laughing and tell her what he was laughing about. Finally, Coop told Naomi the significance of the gift.

"Awe! That is so sweet," she gave K.T. a hug.

"That really is," Coop agreed and gave him a big hug as well.

Gail went next, she gave Coop and Naomi a big box and they opened it together. It had matching photo albums, and a his and hers set of love journals.

They were overwhelmed, "Wow!" Their love story would be captured and preserved in these photo albums and journals. They both hugged Gail and thanked her. Gail pulled a smaller box from her pocket that she had for K.T. He opened it and there was a small photo album with pictures of her from a newborn baby up to the present.

As they all started to get up, K.T. stopped them, "Hold up. I've got a little something, too." He pulled out a small box. Gail opened it up and pulled out a beautiful set of pearls.

"They're gorgeous," she held them up for everyone to see then put them back in the box neatly and gave K.T. a long embrace.

"Okay, you guys can go ahead and turn the game on," Tyra clicked the T.V. on. "I know you're dying to watch it."

"Yes!" They each jumped to a good spot on the couch. The ladies prepared dessert and they all sat around the living room, watched the game, and ate it.

Out of the blue, Coop asked, "By the way, what did you ever find out about our friend, Reggie Banks?"

The ladies were abnormally quiet, as if something was wrong. He looked at each of them. Finally, he told Naomi to tell him what was going on and he wanted to know everything. "I know you won't lie to me," he told her, really putting the pressure on her.

"Why me?" Naomi tried not to look at him.

"Please," he said softly.

"Look guys," interrupted Elaine, "the only reason we hadn't told you is because we didn't want to spoil anything for you before your tryouts."

"Spoil anything?" Serge looked concerned. "Now, we are concerned; the way you're holding out on us."

Bug jumped in, "Is somebody going to tell us what's going on?"

"Okay, but don't get upset with us," Bunny finally broke. "Turns out this Mr. Banks is the head of the league; looks like he was doing some scouting early."

"What!" Coop laughed.

"The what?" Serge questioned.

"That's good news!" Tipp bragged, "He got a chance to see that arm I got, just in case I freeze up at the tryouts."

"So, you're not nervous?" Bunny asked them.

"Nervous? No, more like relieved," Coop replied. "I may be a little nervous during the tryouts. But I was bound to be, anyway."

The guys all shouted, "Yeah!" and demonstrated how good they will look running their plays.

Tyra ran, got the camera, and took pictures of the guys. Then Serge took over the role of photographer. The ladies cheered and posed for some pictures themselves. Serge handed the camera to Bug to catch a picture of him and Tyra. They each took pictures together and clowned around. Soon, they heard soft music playing. Tyra had slipped out and put on some music.

"Oh no!" the men moaned, not again, but they couldn't resist. They started to slow dance.

A loud voice interrupted the romance, "Man, did you see that?" One of the guys caught an incredible play on the T.V. The outburst caused everybody to forget about dancing and turned their attention to the T.V.

The women gave in without a fight and decided to watch the game with them. Of course, when the game was over, the women talked the men into watching a movie with them. It was only fair. By the time the movie was over, the only person awake was Coop. He thought about waking everybody up, but then figured there was no harm in joining them. So, he snuggled up next to Naomi, and fell asleep, too.

Coop was the first one awake at sunrise, and he made sure everyone was up along with him. They all agreed to go to church together. After church, they all weighed in. Their three months were almost up. It was their last week to train before the tryouts and to reach their goals.

Naomi agreed to go first. She closed her eyes as she stepped on the scale.

"Yes!" Coop shouted. "You're in there, baby." She lost exactly thirty pounds.

"Thanks to all of you," Naomi then pointed directly at Coop, "and especially you." She reached out and gave Coop a big hug and kiss.

Tyra went next. She held her breath as she stepped up.

"Yeah!" Serge yelled. "Thirty and two pounds," he picked her up off the scale and gave her a big hug. "And you look great!"

Bunny went after Tyra. She held her hands together, said a quick prayer, and she stepped up.

"Alright, Bunny!" Bug celebrated. "You did it, baby!" She screamed and gave Bug a big hug and kiss.

Tipp gestured for Elaine to go next. Elaine was uneasy, "Oh, I can't do this." She almost shed tears and quickly turned into Tipp's arms, "I'm not ready, Tipp."

"It's okay," Tipp comforted her, "I understand."

The others realized how serious it was for her and offered their support.

"We'll weigh in later," Tipp decided.

"Either way, you win," Coop told Elaine. "You got a man who's gonna love you with all his heart. And you've done great, even if you didn't lose the whole thirty pounds. You've come a long way."

"Thank you," she told Coop trying to pull herself together.

Finally, Gail went, not wanting to let go of K.T.'s hand. But she did. Everyone was quiet for a minute until she opened her eyes to see why they were so quiet. She lost thirty-seven pounds.

12

Final Outcome

That week they all stuck to their training as usual, and the guys got together every night for football practice. They felt great. Finally, the day had come.

Elaine, knowing how much she wanted to reach her goal, too had worked out extra hard, and was sure to eat good the entire week. Early Saturday morning, she got up and weighed herself, alone in her house. She screamed to herself when she realized she had lost thirty-five pounds. She couldn't wait to call Tipp.

Tipp had been up pacing. He was very nervous about tryouts, but Elaine didn't realize it, and blurted out her good news as soon as he answered the phone. Tipp tried not to let his nervousness show and congratulated her, "I'm proud of you, baby. So, you're going to be there tonight, right?" he asked her.

"Wouldn't miss it," she told him. "Either way, you're already a winner," she repeated Coops words, "You've got a woman who's gonna love you with all her heart. And you've come a very long way, even if you don't." She interrupted herself, "Well, you're wonderful and you're my winner, my quarterback, my starting player, my - "

He cut her off and laughed, "Okay! Thanks, babe." He said more softly, "I'll see you tonight."

They all acted like they didn't know Reggie Banks was the head of the league, shook his hand, and headed for the field. The ladies watched intensely as they got hit, hit the other players, threw passes, ran for touchdowns, and more. It was exciting. Each of them had on their new lucky shirts.

After the game, Mr. Banks officially told them who he was. He said he would give them a call the next day personally, one way or the other, with the results.

They all waited anxiously with the ladies by their sides.

"Man! What's taking him so long?" Bug said in frustration.

"What's up with you guys?" Tyra asked. "You were the best things on the field. If you didn't make it, you don't want to play on that team."

"She's right," confirmed Coop. "We had our stuff together; all of us."

"Yeah! What are we sweating? Let's celebrate!" Serge suggested. "Get the popcorn and the glasses. Let's have a toast."

They all picked up on Serge's enthusiasm and cheered, "Yeah!" They got the glasses, poured orange juice, and Coop began the toast, as they all joined in.

"To success!"

"To friends!"

"To winners!"

"To God!"

Before they could hold up their glasses again, the phone rang.

"I've got it," Serge jumped over the couch to get to the phone. As soon as he realized it was Reggie, he signaled everybody.

"Can you guys make practice two nights a week?" Reggie asked.

"Yes!" Serge shouted into the phone. Everyone's excitement built up in the background. He calmed them down long enough to finish the phone conversation, then hung up. "We made it!" he shouted. "Practice on Mondays and Wednesdays, games will begin in May." They cheered some more.

Bug managed to get Bunny to himself, "I'd really like to make the engagement official. I'd like to marry you, Bunny. I love you and I'm gonna need a good woman beside me. What do you say?" He dropped to one knee and pulled out a ring.

"Yes!" She pulled him up and kissed him, "I love you, too."

The same idea ran through Serge's mind, "Miss Thang," he smiled at Tyra, "what do you say we change that name from Miss Lady to Mrs. Henderson? Do you think you could be interested in a player like me?" he asked.

"Just what are you asking, exactly?" Tyra teased and looked down at his knees. "I'm trying to say I don't want to be alone," he acted like he didn't know what she was hinting at. Then getting serious, he pulled out a ring and dropped down on one knee, "I'm trying to say, I love you and that I want you for my wife, if you'll have me."

"You sure you want this thang," she teased, trying not to cry. But she couldn't help it.

He held her in his arms, realizing she was happy, but still wanted confirmation, "So, are you gonna just leave me hanging?" he asked her after a few moments.

"No," she said, "I mean, yes! Yes! I would love to be Mrs. Player. I mean Mrs. Henderson," she said.

Coop interrupted their moment, and broke them up, "What's this? We're gonna have another group joining us?" he asked them.

"We're in!" Serge laid his hand on Coop's.

"We're in, too," Bug added his hand on theirs.

"Yeah!" K.T. yelled and stacked his hand on top of the pile.

Tipp pulled Elaine off to the side, "You know we should have been first, but I've heard it said, *save the best for last.* You know I'm not doing this because of everybody else. I really want to be with you. But it would be nice to go through the process with the others. So, would you please be my wife?" he asked with sincerity.

"For as long as we both shall live," she responded wholeheartedly. Before they could get a chance to kiss, the rest of the gang busted in on them, and they all celebrated together.

The men went on to play amateur football on the same team. The women continued to sing together and impress the crowds. Their weddings were on the same day, confusing the poor preacher. Since the women were already established in their own places, the men moved in with them. They rented their house to five young men, who were on their own for the first time, fresh out of college, just like themselves when they first moved in. They each joined the church, and the choir. Naomi became pregnant in less than a month.

Every year, they all continue to challenge each other by keeping their tradition of making New Year's Resolutions. They are pushed out of their comfort zones to advance their lives. Even the New Year's Resolutions that seem silly at first, always work out for their best.

About the Author

Babette Bailey is a five-time published worldwide author. Each of her unique works share the totality of her heart in different ways. From poetry to expounding on Biblical principles, as they pertain to women and God's desire for the family, to guided motivational life enriching devotionals, and now relatable humorous thought-provoking fiction exuberating relationships.

You and your loved ones will be positively impacted by her work, which is available in the form of books, personalized poetry for all occasions, calendars, and household decor.

If you need help telling *your* story, contact Babette for a ghostwriting consultation.

Please contact Babette Bailey directly for personalized poetry, calendars, household decor, and ghostwriting services:

writeforyourevent@gmail.com

Search your preferred online book retailer for additional works by Babette Bailey:

Additional Works

November 16, 2020

A Glimpse Into My Heart is a collection of poems sparked by many different people, events, hopes, dreams, issues, and a lot of other things that have touched & impacted Babette's heart in different ways.

Just like our lives, like a good song, or like a fresh new idea that could go on and on in our minds, these glimpses are meant to open the heart, gently lift the heart, and bring a spark to the heart that will go on and on.

Babette is glad to have this opportunity to touch your heart by sharing her heart with you. You will not only be able to relate to many of the poems in *A Glimpse Into My Heart*, but you will be inspired, encouraged, lifted up, smile, and even laugh.

Babette Bailey is the mother of three now adult children and grandmother of five. She is the 9th born of ten brothers and sisters.

After writing privately for many years, the time has now come to give a *A Glimpse Into My Heart* to the world.

May 9, 2021

So many times, we feel like we've heard it all before; we've got it all together; we know what we're doing; we're equipped and ready; or like everybody is wrong, except us.

We have even experienced times when we didn't want to hear another teaching, another preaching, another prophesy, or another video. We didn't want to read another book, another article, or another story. And we surely didn't want to talk about it anymore!

I want to encourage you to give it another try! Gather the women in your life, and let's embark on a continuous journey together to develop the *Ladies First* approach to life. This book is a compilation of life experiences, Scriptural truths, and authentic thoughts on matters of the heart.

December 21, 2021

Babette Bailey authentically shares her heart in her newest book of poetry, *Poetic Inspirations*. You are guaranteed to find encouragement, laughter, reasons to celebrate, and good ol' fashion unapologetic advice within these pages.

As you take a deep refreshing poetic breath, you will be inspired, renewed, and refreshed. There are tremendous amounts of love, strength, and positive wholesome messages in this book, heartfeltly prepared to be absorbed by women and men of all ages.

Next Chapter (excerpt)

You grew from just an infant, went from crawling to standing
From mumbling to chanting, from bouncing to standing
You learned to read and write, learned wrong from right
Learned to stand and fight, learned to embrace your plight
You've gone from chapter to chapter, from one situation to the next
From one song to another, you've always given your best
You've served and you've sacrificed, you put in your time and labor
You're about to begin the next chapter,
You're about to start your next adventure . . .

February 14, 2023

Too often we take our covering for granted, until we realize how much we need it. Have you ever found yourself groping for the cover you pushed off during the night?

The design and power of godly coverings are clearly explained in this transparent book. Babette shares her heart, life experiences, and insight, while encouraging us to apply this practical life enhancing concept to better our relationships and live an abundant life.

The thoughts and what I want to portray most about *Uncovered*, are how easy it is to take for granted having a covering, and the devastation we often overlook that can result when we're uncovered. And no matter what season we're in, where we are in the world, or who we are; we all need to be covered. I think it's one of those things we don't think enough about until we realize we are without a covering. I don't think we realize how much we need to be covered until we start to mature and understand our nakedness, our vulnerability, our aloneness, and all the affects that can arise from being uncovered, as well as other major and lasting impacts it can have on our lives.